Seeker of Horizons

Massoud Abbasi

Copyright © 2014 by La Rayan Publishing. All Rights Reserved.

All rights reserved. No part of this publication may be reproduced, distributed, or transmitted in any form or by any means, including photocopying, recording, or other electronic or mechanical methods, without the prior written permission of the publisher, except in the case of brief quotations embodied in critical reviews and certain other noncommercial uses permitted by copyright law. For permission requests, email the publisher, addressed "Attention: Permissions Coordinator," at the address below.

info@larayan.com
www.larayan.com

Ordering Information:
Quantity sales. Special discounts are available on quantity purchases by corporations, associations, and others. For details, contact the publisher at the address above.

The situations in this book are inspired by true events yet the characters are fictional and do not represent any real persons.

Printed in the United States of America

Dedication

For my father, Ali Abbasi, whose spirit was with me as I penned each page. May he rest in peace.

Massoud Abbasi

Table of Contents

Prologue vii

Forlorn in London 1
Culmination of a Crisis 19
The Dream 41
Back in Time 55
Affinity 69
Paradise Lost 85
Vengeance 101
New Hope 115
The Revelation 131
The Truth 149
The Rain 165
Childhood Streets of Tehran 173
All is Not Lost 189

Prologue

Have you ever looked up at a flock of birds flying into the far-off distance above you? Does not the same human spirit that has led us across oceans and mountains vie with these noble creatures of the sky as they flock inexorably towards some great horizon in the distance to which they are drawn? Does not the same majesty that compels these graceful animals forward compel us towards our impossibilities? Do we not all root and cheer for them as they soar, saying, "Fly on, brave pioneers and aeronauts of the spirit. Keep gracing the pressure of the air that hugs itself under your foliage and lifts you like a full moon lifts the oceans. Fly, fly towards a heavenly goal, and in so doing, win a great victory, win infinity and eternity."

This is, after all, why the journey is more important than the destination: The destination is endless; it does not exist. And someday, like these birds, each one of us will have to stop, but the quest does not cease there. That day, we will watch others continue forward – crawling, walking, climbing, and flying – and this will be our solace, those of us that are grounded. Our hearts will flutter just enough to say a prayer for those whose hearts now beat with vigour, saying with them as they vanish into the horizon, 'Keep going, my friends, keep going. It is near, and when you have reached it, you will see ever newer horizons emerge before you, and these also you will seek, but until then, keep going." There are, after all, no endings in life, only beginnings. Begin once more, today.

Whence did this idea of a horizon emerge? It was born of absolute love and adoration of objects that were above us, but also within us – the sun, the clouds, the stars, those items above the terrestrial realm that must have long created a yearning for wings amongst our kind. Our yearning for these things lifted our other faculties out of a silent slumber and into active mechanics. We were thus led towards these divine bodies, these tantalizing slices of heaven, whose fleeting essence none can resist, like the aroma of a flower that we sniff over and over again. Yes, horizons, ever receding ones, the first group of humans must have seen these distances and these birds that traversed them, these troubadours of the skies, and came to realize that where we stand now is not where we are confined to remain. That who we are today shall not necessarily define us tomorrow. Are we not after all propelled forward by these things, we horizon lovers, we purveyors of those things within us, above us, beyond us?

We seek new horizons because present ones expire and become old. After all, there is no beauty in something that lasts forever. This is why we adore life, precisely because we know it must end. Perhaps this is why we are such horizon seekers. Perhaps the search and journey is the enclosing of the shell of incompleteness that defines us. Where we lack within, we see fulfillment without, in the form of ever greater and richer things of and in the world. Imagine how many fantastical notions were dreamt by the first pioneers of flight or those of the sea, and conversely, how many thunderous claps of cold, hard reality and failure were felt and experienced by them on their maiden voyages, all in pursuit of horizons.

It is not through answers, but by questions which we seek and attain ever newer and loftier horizons. Our curious essence as beings vies with that of those flocks of birds flying far off into the unknown. These noble creatures, elevated above the earthly realm by destiny, fly with a great innate purpose in their loins, ever higher, ever further towards the horizon. As they do, they sing hymns and praise their existence, never questioning the path before them nor the destination ahead of them, but rather holding fast to the faith in their hearts that leads them such. Devoid of this faith, they would lose their compass and their way; it is the same with us. Hold fast then to your faith, whatever it may be. It will always guide you home.

Dreams are the greatest of horizons, and though they may be fantastical and of the mind, they can become reality and of the body. They can be achieved collectively, if they cannot be achieved individually. Perhaps the most beautiful of dreams are the ones that embody 'many' as opposed to 'one'. What good is a thing if it is not divisible and shareable with others? In fact, what matters if our dreams are achieved by you or me, today or tomorrow? It is the journey and the firm conviction that they will be achieved one day by us as a family, as a flock, that is, of real value and significance. Every great dream and horizon ever sought out and reached in our history, whether spiritual or scientific, has been drawn by one and achieved by another. So may it be with us. Strident and strong towards the future, our eyes piercing forward, our aim resolute, our destiny within our control. "Where does one horizon end and another begin?" some may ask. Tell them all horizons are one, and one horizon is all. In the final accounting of things, it is not where or what we seek, but that we seek that matters for us, we seekers of horizons…

Chapter 1:
Forlorn in London

My flight was scheduled for 10:30 p.m. The red eye was the only option. At least this way, there would not be another night of waiting to find out my fate. An old mentor of mine used to tell me, "Never make decisions in haste." It may have all sounded inane and hopeless to others, my decision to pursue her, but what did that matter to me? Everyone must follow his or her heart. The passing of my father recently had made me realize that life is truly too short to spend caught up in regrets and missed opportunities. Despite the fact that he was not a good father, nor a good man, I had still wanted to speak to him on several occasions, but never did get around to it and now regretted not doing so, as it was too late. He was gone forever. It wasn't too late with her, however, I hoped at least. Often, we only appreciate something or someone when we have lost them. I suppose that made sense. It is, after all, only through absence that we become aware of presence, and through death that we gain an appreciation for life.

I had spoken with my mother, who was not happy that I was going to London, and my sister Simona, who was completely against it. At least my mother offered me her blessings and prayers. Those are sacred things when they come from a mother. Popping another clonazepam to help me relax, I hoped I wasn't developing an addiction to these anxiety pills. There is no shortage of pills nowadays to help us alleviate the stress of modern life.

Seated at the back of the plane in a window seat, something I didn't like, I placed my bag on the overhead compartment, slamming it shut hard enough that it made a loud noise, revealing my disgruntled state. That's what happens when you check in last, I thought to myself. We were no more than an hour into the flight when I began to have an uneasy feeling about the whole trip and started to experience anxiety and have second thoughts. What if she refuses to see me? What if she isn't with her cousins? What if she doesn't give me another chance?

Shaking my head, as if that was going to help, I tried to eliminate these thoughts, but I wasn't able to and I caught myself spiraling into negative thinking and self-doubt. Sitting beside the window and two other passengers didn't help either; the arm of the man beside me constantly jostled with mine. I finally got up and moved around to get some air. Stepping into the aisle, the plane experienced a small drop just then and I felt a few shakes, startling me and the other passengers. The captain spoke over the speakers, "Ladies and gentlemen, we're approaching some rough patches ahead and will be experiencing some headwinds and modest turbulence. Please take your seat and fasten your seatbelts until you have been further instructed."

That was a welcome distraction, and I quickly made my way down the aisle towards the back and the restrooms, feeling dizzy and nauseous. The head stewardess saw me and said, "Please take a seat right away, Sir." I merely looked back at her, but said nothing as I wasn't feeling well, and I rushed into the bathroom, opening the door by slamming into it with my body. The turbulence was becoming more pronounced, and I was thrown around slightly as I closed the door behind me and locked it just as the stewardess knocked and repeated herself to me. "I don't feel well, damn it!" I yelled back at her, looking up with disdain and surprising myself with the tone of my voice. It worked, as she seemed to disappear. It's usually not that simple with women.

The bathroom wasn't exactly spacious. Coupled with the tight space, my nausea, and the turbulence, it was a perfect recipe for the spins, and right then, I helplessly crouched down towards the toilet, placing my hands on either side, and vomited. After a few moments, I got up, rinsed my mouth, and threw some cold water on my face. Putting down the toilet seat, I sat down. The turbulence had not yet abated, and I was starting to feel sick again from all the shaking and movements of the plane. Closing my eyes and grimacing, I prayed it would stop, as this was all starting to feel like a bad nightmare and an ominous sign for the trip.

"Sir, are you alright?" It was the stewardess again. Looking up, I managed a quick response, "I'm fine, thanks." But I wasn't fine, and I sat there, staring at myself in the mirror, hands clasping the cold plastic frame of this washroom, and wondering how I had reached such a low point in my life. My face frightened me at this moment. Flush red cheeks, veins protruding, my eyes looked incredibly tired, hollow like pockmarks on old country roads. Who the hell was I looking at?

Just then, my weathered and heavy visage triggered a recall of a memory, a traumatic incident that transpired in my younger years far too often. I was 11 or 12 years old and in a similar situation, hiding in the bathroom from my father. "Open this door, right now, or I will break it in, Moshe!" I had left a bowl of soup in the microwave for much longer than required, and it had combusted all over inside. Producing a loud noise which my father had heard from the living room, he came running into the kitchen with that angry and vicious look on his face that terrorized my family for most of our lives. "What the hell was that?" he yelled, which my mother, who was also worried about the imminent outcome, tried to defer his attention from. "Nothing, it was nothing," she claimed nervously, visibly shaking as she walked over towards me.

But he wouldn't relent and sensed my fear as I stood unable to look him in the eyes; he knew something had happened. Any excuse for him to administer a beating. He came closer to the microwave where I was standing petrified and opened it, viewing the complete mess I had created. He then looked at me with his scorched, diabolical eyes, and I looked at his with those of a child's. This brief, silent exchange between two souls was abruptly ended shortly thereafter, as he slapped me so hard with his right hand that my whole body shifted and hit the cupboard, as if I was some bag thrown onto a lorry with no concern.

"Don't touch him, you son of a bitch. He's just a kid!" I heard my mother shouting at my father from behind him. You don't talk like that to a man like my father. He turned around, moved forward, and did the same thing to her, except more than once, and in a moment of abject fear and shock, I ran down the hall to the washroom, locking myself inside, sitting on the toilet seat, and praying for some miracle as I had so many times before. One was not forthcoming; it never was.

A moment later, after some commotion in the kitchen, I felt and heard the floor shake beneath me as my father stormed down the hallway. "Open this God damned door, boy," he said rather angrily, his voice loud and eerie as a crow's in an open, empty field. "Leave him alone, you leave him alone," I could hear my mother yell at my father. I heard him walk away back towards the kitchen, surely to shut her up for good. A monster needs silence to conduct his work after all. Hearing a heavy thud shortly after, a great tremor reverberated throughout my small and delicate frame. I knew exactly what that noise was. All these noises of horror were long familiar to me. They were ingrained from long ago. The audible sounds of my father taking out his rage and anger on my poor mother, a woman half his size who had endured one too many such injustices throughout the greater part of her life, just to help assuage a troubled man's diseased and tortured conscience. The human psyche can be a sordid and sad thing.

Trembling and crying, wiping the tears away with both my hands at once, I got up and walked towards the door, taking light gentle steps. My legs moved slow, thick with the molasses of fear. The door seemed like it was a mile away. I felt horrible and guilty that my actions had led to my mother having to endure their repercussions. I wished I had never been born in those moments, a heavy thought for a child. We've all thought this thought at one point or another in life. Opening the door ever so slightly, lest I should draw his attention, I could hear her screaming, "Let me go, let me go, let me go!" He must have been dragging her by her hair as he did on many occasions. I knew this because the sound was getting further away from me, though I felt her pain more closely with each wail.

Overcoming my paralysis, I displayed a courage that should not be required of a young boy at such a tender age and opened the door fully and stepped into the hallway. Walking tepidly down it and into the kitchen, I witnessed an image that would forever be seared into my consciousness and would always haunt me: my father standing above my mother, towering her like a statue, her on the floor, face bruised and bloodied from forehead to lips, crying on the corner near the aged, clunky, yellow refrigerator. She was sobbing in pain and sadness at her daily plight. Lips quivering, knees buckling, I could barely feel my body, but I managed to utter a few words ever so softly, which I believed might lift the burden from her and onto myself: "It was me."

My father turned around and looked at me, his face distraught, yet still severe with sickness and disease like a rotting apple. Regardless of how tortured or damaged a man may be, he cannot feel good about doing such things to another person, especially to a woman. Ultimately, we hurt others, because deep down, we wish to hurt ourselves. We project ourselves onto others, then attack them, because it's more convenient this way. My father continued staring at me, seemingly also paralyzed by the situation, as he breathed heavily, but did not move.

By now, my sister Nas had come out of her room and grabbed me from behind, pulling me away towards her room, while I stared first at my dad, our eyes connecting for a moment in which I could see the wretchedness of his being, naked and bare before my young eyes like a fruit without its peel, followed by a quick glance at my mom, whose eyes spoke of eternal love and eternal pain like spring and autumn. A second later, I was out of sight and in my sister's room, where we would sit huddled in fear that the monster was not yet done with his work. It was a warm summer day from what I recall, but I shivered as if I sat naked on a barren winter plane in January.

"Sir?" I heard quite pronounced, followed by several loud knocks. I snapped out of it immediately and realized that I had slipped into my subconscious and was experiencing a very lucid flashback in the bathroom of the airplane. "Sir, are you alright?"

I shook it off and finally responded, "Yes, yes, I'm fine. Just fell asleep, that's all. Be right out." Standing up, I took several deep breaths to relieve myself of this small nightmare that had just flashed in front of my eyes. I flushed the toilet, threw some more water on my face, and opened the door to an audience: a few passengers who had been waiting, and some stewards who were clearly worried about me. "I'm very sorry. I wasn't feeling well," I said, slightly embarrassed with my head down, unable to look anyone in the eye. I headed back to my seat, took another pill, and tried my best to sleep for the remainder of the flight. Perhaps this was all a mistake.

It was early morning when we finally touched down in London. Standing there for a moment at the airport, trying to take it all in, I realized just how much had happened in the span of only a few days. Was this all really happening? Did I actually love this girl this much, or was my sister right, that I was vulnerable and could not stand being alone, especially at such a tumultuous time in my life? I convinced myself it was the former, not the latter. Maybe she was right, but I was in no mood to entertain such a thought. Besides, how could

I be lonely? I was so popular and well connected; I knew that was bullshit, however, deep down. Nowadays, we may know more and more people thanks to cities and technology, but it is all so superficial that many almost feel as if they know no one anymore, not even themselves. I felt just this way lately. I looked around the airport, thousands of beings coming and going. The flashback in the plane had not yet left me. Melancholy, sighing, I felt a sadness and longing for my poor mother. She had lived under that man's iron fist for almost 30 years, something I could not even fathom; perhaps I just didn't want to.

I was looking forward to seeing him once again, my old friend. We were close back in Toronto, having gone to school together, then both entering the field of finance with the same firm upon graduation. Alexander was African-American with Nigerian roots. Tall and athletic, Alexander was well comported in all respects. He seemed to have it all together, something I envied him for. He had moved to London just a couple of years ago for a work opportunity, and this was our first reunion since. It was comforting to know that I had a good friend in town during all this.

Taking one of the distinct London cabs to Alexander's flat in The City, I had a fair 35-40 minutes of daydreaming time on the highway to London from Heathrow. Isn't that after all what cab rides are about, daydreaming? I spent it practicing what I would say upon coming face-to-face with her. I went through various permutations of the same: "Anastasya, I love you, I made a mistake, I was going through a lot, I was grieving my father, etc." I had one particular line picked out I felt was poetic, but couldn't quite complete it. I slammed my hands in frustration on the front seat, blurting "Damn it" and drawing the attention of the driver, who looked at me using his mirror.

"You alright, mate?" he said to me in a distinct, Cockneyed accent.

"Yes, I'm fine," I said to him in response. "Just thinking about something."

There was a pause.

"You thinking about a woman?" he said with a smirk and raised brow, drawing my attention once again. I stared blankly at him. What the hell, I thought, I wasn't coming up with anything worthwhile to say to her anyways.

"I am," I responded, curious, welcoming advice, or just a distraction. Just then, my body jumped off the seat, nearly hitting my head on the ceiling as the car drove over something.

"Ah, sorry, mate, didn't notice that speed bump."

Giving him a jagged look, he wasn't paying attention to me. Why was I even paying attention to him? I needed to be prepared for when I confronted her, I thought again. I went through it once more, practicing various things I could say to her, but just as I was formulating something, we came to a full stop at an area in the city because of construction.

"Ah, blimey," the driver, a short, stocky man with a bald head, French cap, and light brown goatee, said.

"What's wrong?" I said to him, looking on curious.

"Construction. This whole city is under it. How much more can they jam in here?"

His comment reminded me of Toronto, my beloved home city that was itself undergoing dramatic changes. A "New York in the making" is how I liked to view it. I turned my head towards the window, looking outside at the artifices of yet another major city. I was weary of this glass and cement jungle that I and many others had simply accepted as humanity's only lot and option today. Had this really become our destiny as a species? Perhaps we should just return to nature, to the wild? Wild thoughts, I whispered to myself.

"Just be honest with her," I heard him say to me, interrupting my train of thought yet again.

Irritated, I rolled my eyes and replied, "What?"

He looked at me again and said, "Tell her how you feel, what you want, what you'll do, and nothing more."

I was receiving love and relationship advice from an Englishman, a taxi driver in London. I couldn't help but chuckle.

"Yeah, sure. I will," I responded. "How much longer until we're there?"

"We'll be there in a jiffy, mate," was the response.

Not soon enough for me. The moment of truth was near and I was hopeful. I had to be; what choice did I have? Hope is a good thing, but a bad strategy. I closed my eyes and took a deep breath. What is that the English are so fond of saying? Keep calm and carry on. Indeed.

I had been attempting to reach her for several hours from Alexander's apartment. It was several hours before I finally received a response from her. My phone lit up with a message with her name. My eyes opened up wide, as if I was seeing an apparition. I felt a glimmer of hope about it all again, practically giddy. Had I become this desperate? The hope quickly faded however. The message was not in my favour. "We are done. You left me alone for weeks, after I was there to support you during the hardest time of your life when your father passed." I raised my head at this point, realizing what else was coming. "Forget all the other things that you did to me. I overlooked those, but abandoning me, leaving me alone at such a time, how can I ever trust you again? Please leave and let me be. I'm sorry, but you shouldn't have come here." A tear slid down my cheek. "If you love me, you would respect my request. Love is selfless, not selfish, and you never understood that. Goodbye." She had said that line to me before, and she was right. I began to panic; my breathing became heavy as my chest heaved. I resorted to another clonazepam. I had lost her for good.

Pride does not relent easily, especially when it is puffed up as mine usually is. I had come this far, and I simply had to see her. Besides, she loved me, and love doesn't fade quickly. She was just angry, I convinced myself. I knew where she was staying, her cousin's flat in Knightsbridge. We had spent a Christmas there together. I knew London well enough, so I took the underground there.

It was still afternoon when I reached my destination. I'm quite sure she would be home and would eventually step out; she liked taking walks. It was worth an attempt anyways. Arriving at the building, I forgot that it was a gated one. I tried to think of a clever way inside; I knew the apartment after all, but it seemed too difficult and risky and I did not want to scare her off. Luckily, there was a small boutique hotel next door that had a view directly on her building's front entrance. I decided I would sit there and wait it out, as if on a stakeout.

It was just over two hours before she finally emerged. I caught a glimpse of her slender figure right away. Her auburn hair, light skin tone, sharp chiseled cheekbones, and piercing hazel eyes, all just as I remembered. Wearing high heeled black boots and a tan leather jacket, she walked with purpose past the doorman, to whom she threw a smile. I was frozen for a moment, her image seeming like a mirage to me. I hopped off the couch instantly, like a coiled spring, and began after her when I heard the attendant call me.

"Sir. Your belongings." I looked at him, then at my items, stepping back to grab the bouquet of luscious, red roses, the golden box of chocolates, and the small bag from a local jeweler where I had purchased a modest, silver engagement ring.

"Thank you," I blurted out as I hurried through the lobby doors and out the boutique.

"Good luck," I heard faintly as I exited.

I saw her, maybe 100 metres ahead, pacing along at a brisk rate, as if eager to arrive somewhere, my beautiful Anastasya. I kept my distance, but did not lose sight of my girl just ahead of me. She was so close, yet so far. Doesn't love always feel this way?

I followed her for several more blocks. I practiced what I would say to her during this time quietly to myself. The sweat and hurried breathing indicated much about my state. It's easy to shun someone over the phone; technology removes accountability and feeling. In person, however, it's another matter. She couldn't resist me in person, I was sure of it. All I needed to do was lock eyes with her and they would speak the infinite. I smiled at this thought, at the idea of staring into her soul again.

Finally reaching a narrow, cobblestone alleyway, I stood far back and let her pass before I followed. Doing so eventually, I followed suit quickly and found myself in a leisurely area that seemed like a small slice of bohemia. I was surrounded by cafes, restaurants, and people. She walked into a café across the street from me. I had her cornered now; here was my chance.

She would be moved by all of my efforts, I convinced myself, as I swiftly moved through a variety of people, city dwellers, and young professionals, each with a storybook of their hopes and dreams and successes and failures in the big city. I finally landed directly across the street from her. She was sitting down by the window, looking at her phone. The sight of her elated me, and I felt butterflies in my stomach that only love produces. I felt alive once more.

What would I say to her, I thought now? What if she got up and stormed out? No, she wouldn't do that. We shared too much history together. She'll hear me out at least. "Anastasya, I'm sorry, I don't know why I..." No, that wasn't it. "Baby, I'm really and truly sorry and sad about us, but..." Shit, I blurted out, frustrated and unable to compose a decent line. I decided to just let it come out on its own naturally; that's usually the best method anyways, speaking from the heart.

I looked both ways before crossing the street, but just before I reached the sidewalk of the other side, I froze up on the road like dried tar and my jaw dropped. I felt a chill move down my spine. A heavy cloud surrounded me, spreading itself over me. I wish I was imagining what had just happened, but I was not. A young man had approached her from out of the blue and kissed her on the lips, briefly, but passionately, and sat down across from her, smiling amorously. She seemed happy about it all. I felt like a cog had been inserted into my heart. Closing my eyes, hoping perhaps it was all a dream, I opened them again to a nightmare. My eyes welled up. I felt the disbelief of a heretic at it all. I even forgot that I was standing on a road just then. Reality finally set in when I saw a faint reflection of myself in the window of the cafe. Now I knew it was real, I could see myself within it. Who was I anymore, though? Who was she? How does someone you love one moment become a stranger the next? How could she move on so quickly? Did I mean so little to her?

My lips quivered as I watched her smile and chat with this stranger. My eyes began to bleed tears. I dropped the gifts on the ground. I took one last look at her, knowing this may well be the last time I did so ever again, hoping deep down she might notice me. But sadly, she did not, and I now knew I had truly lost her forever. I wished the ground would swallow me at that very moment.

I had hurried back to Alexander's; it was my place of solace for now. Back upstairs in the flat, devastated, I tried to stop my tears. How could she do this to me? It hadn't been more than a couple of weeks since everything transpired; how could she move on so fast? Was this a product of her character or a product of the times? With the abundance of options and distractions at one's disposal in city life nowadays, even the sturdiest bedrock of love is vulnerable today.

Love, I thought, what the hell is that anyways? How fickle have we become as a people, as a race? Are the memories and experiences we share with others so ephemeral as to be so quickly banished from our hearts and minds? Is this what modern life has made us?

Many things ran through my mind, but one thing was for sure: I could not stay in London any longer. This city reminded me too much of her; she was a native here. Everything about London now became about her, suffocating me. Wiping away my tears and resolving to not succumb to my emotions and feelings, I decided to book my flight back home at once and leave this city right away. In fact, I did not want to return to Toronto at all. I had enough of city life, and I simply couldn't stay in London a minute longer. Reaching into my travel bag for the notebook containing the airline information, my hands slipped on something I did not recognize at first at the bottom of it, but did so quickly once I had pulled them out: my father's folders. I had completely forgotten that I had brought them along with me.

Staring at them as if they were some unknown substance, unsure as to what they contained, I decided to finally open them up and relieve myself of the suspense and mystery. Surely, it couldn't be any worse than what I had just endured. I ripped them open rather aggressively, tearing the package as if I was angry with it. The first envelope contained several very old Turkish magazines of a political nature. The language was foreign to me. There were several notebooks as well, seemingly journals of my father's, small ones, something I did not know he maintained. Interestingly, there were also many pictures, some from the press room where he worked in Tehran as a journalist, some of my family, and some of his colleagues at various times in the past, including ones from his time spent in prison.

I know very little about my father or his life. He was a very private man, but not an ordinary one. I opened up one of his smaller journals, briefly scouring it. Most of it was, of course, in Farsi, which I could not read, but there were some notes in English and French, which I could. My father was fluent in five languages. I always knew my father was a politically active man; you don't get imprisoned, tortured, and almost killed for no reason, but I really did not know all that much more. The truth of his life was probably in here somewhere. I'm sure his secrets also.

Intrigued, I carried them over to the couch and sat down, never taking my eyes off them. Perhaps I could finally get a better sense of the man and why he was the way he was. There was more material here than I thought, and much of it was quite dense and intriguing. Why had he left these with a lawyer in trust, and why had I received them when he passed? When I had first asked my mother about them a couple of days ago back home, she was quiet and tried to persuade me to ignore them. There was a hesitation in her voice, a nervousness of sorts. Why, I thought, rubbing my face in questioning? What information or secrets was contained in these notebooks, these pictures, these documents? Who was it that left me the note that advised me to follow these items to the truth, I wondered now? It was all rather strange and surreal, like some mystery game. Except it was no game; life is no game.

I was interrupted by a call from my youngest sister, Sara, who was checking up on me. What was I to tell her but the truth, and I did. "Just come home," was her response. I wasn't sure what that meant anymore, home. I paused for a moment and glanced at the envelopes.

"Sis, do you know anything about Dad's life that I am not aware of?"

She seemed caught off guard. "I don't understand," she responded.

"Well," I said, "did he have any secrets that I or we are not aware of?"

She went quiet for a moment. "I really don't know what you're talking about, my brother." I believed her, letting out a sigh. "You know none of us knew much about him," she said to me. That was indeed true. His pain, however, had always been mine, and I wore it all too readily, even now. None of my siblings had much of a relationship with him, nor did they feel much compassion towards him, if at all. Who could blame them considering the hell he put us through all our lives?

I was not as indifferent towards him as my other siblings however. I had an affinity to this dark and complicated man. Whether I liked it or not, I was his son and he was my father, and we shared much in common besides just physical characteristics. My one fear had always been that if I did not understand him and the reasons for his turning out the way he did, for what ailed him, that I too would suffer the same fate one day. Those who don't learn from history are doomed to repeat it, after all. Perhaps what I was looking for was in these files? Perhaps I could finally shed some light on this man and where he went off course in life.

"Hello? You there?" I heard my sister saying, snapping me out of my thoughts.

Shaking my head, I placed the phone directly back on my ear and responded, "Yes, sis, I'm right here."

A couple of hours had transpired when I woke, suddenly lying on the couch in Alexander's flat. At first, I could scarcely make out where I was and what I was doing. When I did, I regretted it. Reality had become a nightmare as I recalled the events of the day. My heart sank yet again, and I felt like crawling into a hole and dying. I looked out at the city as I sat up on the stiff leather couch. It was the same as back home: cold, austere, built with efficiency in mind, not life or passion. What was I to do now? Return home with my hat in hand, admitting failure? Then what? Go back to work, submit myself once again to daily corporate service? I was better off going to the emergency room.

I placed my hands on my face, running them up and down in frustration. "God damn it, I yelled. Why me?"

Wiping the moisture from around my eyes, I looked at my phone, realizing I was to rendezvous with Alexander this evening. I fell back on the couch. I was in no mood to speak to anyone, but I had already committed. Maybe it wasn't such a bad idea to meet him. I needed to unload the weight off my back. He already knew some of the story, and I might as well tell him the rest.

"Keep it together, man," I said to myself, sitting up. I forced myself off the couch and to the bathroom, where I washed up. I got ready next. Then I stepped out.

It was just before 8 p.m. when I finally reached the meeting point near a major tube station on the Thames. Waiting for me, I could see him, Alexander. In a sharp, navy blue suit with a loosened tie, he smiled at me as I approached, but it was a restrained one. He knew; I had told him in advance with a text message. "Sorry, mate," he said to me after we embraced one another. "You tried, there is no shame in that." Perhaps he was right.

We walked along the Thames, talking. At times, I would look at him as he spoke and I secretly envied him. He seemed to have it all together: a steady job and a clearly laid-out career path, a comfortable flat, a good partner, a positive outlook on life. Aren't we all looking for these things amidst the chaos? Where do we find them amongst this metropolitan heaviness that we all seem to be crushed under? I did not know. I wish I had it as together as he did. I wish I had it all figured out. Sometimes I felt like everyone else had life figured out but me. It's highly unlikely that's the case, but that's how I felt. If only we could stop comparing our lives to those of others, judging ours by juxtaposing it with theirs. It's a pointless exercise, as no two lives are alike or the same. I wanted to tell him more, tell him about what had happened the last few days back home that had brought me here, but I couldn't do it. It required too much strength, and I had only weakness.

Walking along, both of us quiet, the sun setting ahead of us to the left, I wondered if two souls can ever truly capture and encompass one another. Looking at the sky just then, I thought about the night and the stars. We're like the stars, human beings, in the night sky. Upon a quick glance, we all look incredibly close to one another, but upon further reflection, we realize and remember that often we are infinitely far apart.

We continued walking along the Thames as the sun slowly set on this bustling, world class city that I would forever associate with her. We walked another hour or so. It was quite busy in the central area where we were. The sun was descending below the earth, leaving a golden glow across swathes of the land. What would I do next but go home, I thought to myself. I wasn't ready to face that just yet, there was nothing there for me anymore. What is home? My father was gone and now her, all in the span of a few weeks. Life had me spinning like a loose ball of yarn rolling down a hill. Perhaps I needed to continue the journey. I could use some time alone to reflect on things after all, to make peace with her, to make peace with him, to perhaps look further into his notebooks and the files that were with me and which were on my mind now.

I had always wanted to visit Lake Como in Italy. What better time than now, I thought, as I was already in Europe and not so far away. Solitude can be powerful healer. So can leaving everything and everyone behind for a period of time. Perhaps this was not an end, but a beginning. Whole galaxies are, after all, born in grand explosions and convulsions of stars. Why couldn't the same be true for people, I thought to myself. I needed to figure out my next move. I felt like I was in some grand chess game, except I was playing against myself. I told Alexander that I needed to be alone and would catch up with him later tonight or tomorrow. Of course, he understood, and we parted ways.

Shortly later, I was crossing one of the major bridges that linked the two sides of London together. I was halfway across when I caught a majestic scene and view to my right, which entranced me and left me unable to move and a pure spectator. I placed my hands over the bridge's guardrails and peered out above and ahead. A wide, winding waterway with many boats coming and going, buildings and structures on either side as far as the eye could see, people everywhere moving about in their activities and rituals, and far ahead, deep on the horizon, the resplendent sunset and glow of heaven.

Just as I was caught up in the beauty before me, absolutely present and in the moment, and having temporarily forgotten my troubles, a flock of birds flew past above me in unison, heading into the distance with determination and purpose. I was overcome with a strong and strange sense of déjà vu. Just a couple of days ago, standing on my balcony back home in Toronto, I had witnessed a similar sight and occurrence, which gave me the inspiration to set out towards London in search of Anastasya. Here I stood, witnessing yet again the same thing in London. I am not a superstitious man, but sometimes there are signs we cannot deny and must embrace. We know this first not in our minds, but in our hearts. My heart beat with vigour at just this moment, and I paid attention to it. This seemed to be a sign, and a fateful one at that. What did I have to lose? The city, home, work, people, those things I had grown weary of. Besides, they would always be there if I missed them. I had travelled this far already. I would travel a bit further. Very few of us ever have an adventure or journey in life to call our own. I refused to be such a person. What better time than the present?

It was time for a voyage of self-reckoning. Lake Como beckoned.

Chapter 2:
Culmination of a Crisis

I arrived back at Alexander's flat rather late, right around midnight. I had gotten lost in my thoughts wandering London. Seeing that flock of birds earlier while I stood on the bridge had resonated with me deeply. He was upset that I hadn't called him. Maybe he had a right to be.

"Listen," he said to me in a hush tone, "I'm worried about you, mate." I looked at him and reassured him that he didn't need to be. "We go back, you and I," he said next looking me directly in my eyes. "You can talk to me." I had brushed him off earlier when he tried to inquire, promising him I would explain later, but it was later and he insisted on knowing what had happened back home in Toronto just a couple of days ago that had led to all of this, to my coming to London.

"Talk to me" he repeated himself again, wrinkles forming on his forehead as his eyes widened.

"Don't you have to work in the morning Alexander?" I responded.

He stared at me, sensing my apprehension. "Alright, then," he said as he got up abruptly and walked to the kitchen. I looked on curiously. He grabbed two small glasses, poured some crushed ice in them, then reached above the fridge cabinet and pulled out an old, amber bottle. Squinting, I noticed it was an old bottle of scotch. A smirk of sorts on his face, I chuckled as he strode back towards me.

"Well, you certainly know me well, pal," I said to him. I have a weak spot for scotch, and he knew I couldn't resist it. Is that not what makes a good friend after all, knowing another's weaknesses and being completely accepting of them?

"Now," he said as he poured us both a large serving, "I can tell my boss I was out drinking with the boys in the morning and he'll understand why I'm late." He rolled his eyes up at me, and I smiled. We both laughed and toasted one another, eyes locking in solidarity. I really had no choice any longer. It was time to tell Alexander everything that had happened a couple of days ago back home in Toronto. Slipping into my mind, I began.

I always enjoyed the journey to an airport, as it often meant that I was headed on another voyage. Not this time. I was so anxious I could barely even clear my throat, let alone breathe clearly. This trip was a chase against time, and a chase to catch her before she left to London.

"Could you please drive faster?" I muttered to the taxi driver, an older, darker man likely in his late 40s who had the luck of picking me up this day.

"I'm going as fast as possible, sir," he responded back. "There is police around these parts."

Police, I thought to myself. How are they of my concern right now? What did the law mean to me anymore? Relics of a modern life I no longer cared for and detested. I couldn't lose two people in such a short period of time. I wondered how life could change so quickly, so dramatically from one moment to the next, as I was gazing up at the sky outside my window as if it would provide me with an answer. Just then, my whole body shifted violently as the driver made a certain maneuver. Looking at him using his dangling front mirror, and noticing him looking back at me at the exact same time, we had a moment right then and there, our eyes capturing one another's story in a brief glimpse and exchange of two lives. He could tell how important this was to me. He did not know details, but he knew what he needed to as soon as I had stepped into his cab. My haste and desperation were eminent, and my body language said all that was necessary without saying a word. The body speaks much louder than the mouth.

It was a half overcast day in Toronto, mild, here and there, and sparks of the sun would penetrate openings amongst the clouds and illuminate the landscape in golden colours, much in stark contrast to the colours of my spirit. It didn't escape me that I almost felt like I was in some movie, chasing someone to the airport. Normally, I would paint such things in a sarcastic tone, perhaps quietly thinking to myself, "What a schmuck!" One can truly never know what tomorrow will bring. Everything can change in an instant; it's quite sobering when it happens to you. Where did I fall asleep and go wrong, I thought to myself?

A bump caused my body to jump, bringing me back from my thoughts as we climbed up a ramp and approached the departures zone. Runways to my right full of airplanes taxiing in and out like clockwork, carrying some to their dreams, and others to their nightmares. Pangs of anxiety washed over me like monsoon rains at the thought that she could be in one of them. Pulling out my leather wallet and fumbling it in my hands, I grabbed a hold of it like a jumping fish out of water and pulled out a $100 bill for the driver.

"Here," I yelled, "right here is good. Pull over." I practically threw the bill at him, while throwing myself out of the car before it had even made a full stop. I must have tipped him well.

I never did catch her that day. It was the evening, and I was seated on the window sill of my condo many stories off the ground. Thoughts raced across my mind mercilessly with no end. The sky above me was heavy and charcoal grey with thick clouds, from which a light rain was dropping on the city. The only thing sustaining me at this point was the hope that this was a nightmare from which I would soon wake. That at any moment, she would come running through the front door. I maintained hope. We need hope, especially in our darker moments. It is the light tower in the sea of life, providing guidance and salvation to individuals lost at sea. Hope is necessary, but dangerous, just like love.

Looking at the glass in my hands, cold and stale, I sipped the last bit of my drink in one gulp, grimaced, and turned my attention towards my apartment. It was uncharacteristically messy. Books were strewn about all over the room, many of which I considered treasures of mine, remnants of my undergraduate years, during which I studied philosophy. Later on, I studied finance so that I could make an actual living. This decision still sometimes left me feeling as though I sold myself short, pursuing money instead of passion like so many of us seem to nowadays, thinking we have no choice. That was a mistake on my part, we always have a choice. Life itself is a choice.

I was a successful financial professional, as well as an entrepreneur. I had it all, but none of it seemed to make me happy: money, looks, youth, popularity. These are the things which all of us search for and seek, and I had obtained them at a young age, but they were clearly not enough. They had not satisfied, nor fulfilled me as I had expected them to. I loathed this place, its cubicle-like structure, its mechanical layout and typical, bland design. Here a useless item, there a generic piece of print art. Nothing original here, just another box in the sky, literally, in the ocean of boxes which comprise what we call the modern metropolis or city these days.

I felt a pervasive malaise at this moment, unable to move my body or my mind as if chastened by a straight coat or the tentacles of some monster. What is it people are fond of saying, that when it rains it pours? It seemed true enough. Not only was my father dead, but I was dealing with a messy breakup as well. Painfully cognizant of my losses at this moment, sadness washed over my heart like the sounds of the strings of a violin. I lowered my head in dejection and closed my eyes in defeat.

At this point, the rain was coming down even harder, creating an audible symphony all its own. I began to hear Mozart in my mind. My father appreciated good music. I glanced over at his picture on the mantle. Not a man prone to talk much or show his feelings, whenever he heard any such sounds emanating from my laptop or radio, he would ask me to turn it up. And I would with delight, bringing us together somehow, if even for a brief moment. We were never close, my father and I. In fact, he was really just a father in the literal sense of the term. Nevertheless, his being and ways had a profound effect on me, despite the hardship he put me and my family through all of our lives. The apple may fall and roll away from the tree, but it will always retain the seed of its genesis. An imperious man in physique and demeanour, my father stood out amongst a crowd. Highly educated, refined, an intellectual, he was a tragic figure of the first order. The Greeks would have certainly created a play about him. He was a gifted writer and a prominent journalist in Tehran during the seminal decades of the 1970s and 1980s, during which fundamental regime and cultural revolutions had transpired. He found himself in the middle of a seismic rift in Iranian society. Fearless, resourceful, and with an established and respected voice, he had made his viewpoints and critiques of the prevailing power base widely known, eventually drawing their ire and resulting in his imprisonment in the notorious Evin prison, an Iranian gulag for the intelligentsia from where many intellectuals did not return.

Closing my eyes, I conjured his face: prominent jaw and cheekbones, deep penetrating eyes, partially bald in a fashion that made him look rugged and complex. He had a strong personality, a broody disposition, and an intimidating and heavy aura. One could easily mistake him for an underground type. He was once purportedly a fair man who believed in justice and equality and attempted to use truth through the written word to reveal the inequities of the prevailing system in his beloved homeland. All these things I had mostly heard in passing. In all our lives, me, my mother and my five siblings, two younger brothers and three older sisters, we saw neither justice, nor equality from this tormented, bitter, abusive man.

All of a sudden, I realized Mozart had stopped parading in my mind, replaced instead with tears dripping down my face. I took my eyes off his picture and turned my head away, looking out at the cold and barren city, wondering why he put us through such hell? The absence of an answer to this question has always tortured me. How I wished for natural landscape and sunshine, instead of this austere cement and glass city, this mechanical, modern existence. My father broke the fundamental agreement that should exist between a child and their parent: unconditional love and protection. He betrayed me and my family.

Hearing several loud knocks, I snapped up and out of my thoughts, my head turning to face the door. Who could it be? I did not want to see anyone, but the knocking persisted and became more pronounced, at which time, I decided to slowly walk over and check who it was through the viewing hole. Peering through it, I saw a young man in a dark grey suit with curly long hair and a black rain jacket, holding a black briefcase and a large folder. He looked the part of a hitman. Nervous, I stepped back for a moment, unsure of what to do. Convincing myself I had no reason to be worried, I decided to open the door. Keeping the chain latched, I did so slowly, peering out of the crevice. The young man looked at me askance, as if I was some lunatic, my eyes blood shot and wide open from days of living and dying.

"Mr. Moshe Asham?" he said, questioningly.

"Yes, that's me," I responded.

"I'm from the office of Harvey Katz. Your father was a client and had left this in trust with us," he said as he raised his right arm to show me the two large folders in his right hand. Looking at them, I was dumbfounded, as I had not even known my father had a lawyer.

The young man continued. "He did not specify a receiver at the time, but given that you are his estate executor, legally, it belongs to you." Stepping forward to pass them over to me, I nervously put my hand out, which was visibly shaking, drawing a quick glance by him of confusion as I received them.

"Are you alright?" he asked me next.

"Ah, yes, yes," I whispered as I stared at the envelopes, confused. "Thank you."

"I'm sorry for your loss," he said next. I froze and stared at him with my swollen eyes. I then abruptly shut the door hard on him. Retreating slowly into the living room, envelopes in hand, I was at a loss as to their contents. I didn't even care to know anymore. It was probably financial matters or such. In a fit of frustration, I slammed both the envelopes on the glass coffee table, creating a loud thud.

"Damn paper society, damn bureaucracy, to hell with this bullshit," I yelled, making my way to the kitchen to find my anxiety pills. Swallowing one, I closed my eyes and lifted my head back. A dizziness overcame me and I felt nauseous. I needed some fresh air. Grabbing my black rain jacket and umbrella, I quickly made my way downstairs.

The rain was descending with fury on the city, cleansing it of its filth, if at least for a short while. Walking with my umbrella drawn, bullets of water riddling it above my head, the streets were largely devoid of people. I reflected on my life. Sadly, it was not a particularly joyous or happy one. My family and I had endured our share of hardships and rough times, bumpy roads, and headwinds. We lived under a tyrant of a father. Childhood leaves a lasting mark on a person. Mine had left an indelible imprint on me, along with many scars. The first boy of the family, I was the de facto patriarch of a broken home. My parents did not have much of a relationship. My mom was a simple woman full of love and affection, raised on a farm in the Iranian countryside. She would have settled for the same simple life if she had a choice. Wouldn't we all nowadays? My father was a brilliant intellectual, a man of depth. Like millions of others, we were vagrants for a period of our lives, whilst in transit to the proverbial 'better life' abroad. The journey was dark and treacherous, like life in the trenches.

We made it home, however, arriving in Canada in 1990. We embarked on the same, difficult journey that millions have around the world of restarting over. Here was a new horizon for me and my family, with more freedom and opportunity, but wrought with challenges. Mine was an upbringing of heaviness, of great conflict. I was born to an angel who lived with the devil in a sea of fire in a time of tumult. That is an apt description for the first two decades of my life. How do we survive what happens to us? I think we hope and dream, however dangerous or misleading these things may be. I survived by the distinct, but effervescent scents of the dreams I created for myself. This is, after all, the medicine of the helpless and hopeless – fantasy. It sustains the possibility of the soul's dreams and desires during a period in which the body and spirit cannot satisfy them. We all need something to believe in. Without conviction, fantasy or faith, we are dead.

I reached an intersection and came to a stop. The faint rumble of thunder emanated from afar, but I sensed it coming. Nature's language is subtle, but sure. Looking at the façade of the buildings, for once they seemed lively and welcoming as the rain reflected all the opposing lights onto their surfaces, taking away their regular dreariness. Something poignant struck my eye from across the street, and

I squinted to get a better look. It was a man with a prosthetic arm and leg sitting under the yellow canopy of an entrance to a luxury retail store. Melancholy overcame me at this sight. Nearing him, I noticed there was a small, brown Labrador beside him that had its head down with deep, droopy eyes. Yes, even animals feel.

I stared at this poor soul for a moment, producing a faint smile for him so as to hide any pity. Staring back at me there was no trace of happiness to him, no faint smile. I reached into my pocket for some change, which I passed over. He accepted it and nodded. I noticed above him an ad for a men's sportswear company in which two middle aged, bronze, healthy, looking men, were standing beside their luxury vehicle on the beach. The irony of it all. I felt helpless, as many do, who amidst this great material landscape, see others who seem to have been left out. I left my umbrella behind with him as I noticed the rain was somewhat reaching his perch. It was the least I could do. Nodding again to me, I nodded back and turned away.

Fully exposed to the rain, I crossed the street and headed back home, but was stopped in my tracks by a large plasma screen atop a hotel entrance showcasing the news across the street. I was transfixed at this very moment and slipped into a recurring memory of me watching the news with my father, one of the few things I did with him during my life. He loved watching the news. An intelligent and worldly man and a former prominent intellectual no longer involved, I knew that this was one of the reasons he became so bitter and angry at how life had turned out for him. What is a man without his profession, his passion, after all? Just another mammal. Watching news was his way of remaining in touch with what he once was. We all need to feel important and involved in something bigger and greater than ourselves after all.

Right then, I was startled and immediately pulled out of my daydream by a blaring horn, the screeching of a vehicle, and the headlights of an oncoming bus, which came to an abrupt halt no more than a couple of feet away from me. Drenched, I stood there petrified, as a momentary lapse of consciousness had nearly led to my death.

"What the hell is wrong with you? Are you crazy?" screamed the driver, a large man with a thick, orange beard from the driver's side window. Staring directly at him, eyes wide open and chest heaving, I didn't say anything, but merely walked backward a few steps, blinked finally, and turned around and began running home in haste.

A shiver ran through me as I recalled all this for Alexander. I had gone beyond just telling him how I had reached this point. I was now pouring out my heart to him, along with the intimate details of my life. I looked at my watch; it was nearly 1 a.m.

"Hey, come on, you've got to work tomorrow morning. You don't want to hear this right now," I said as I stood up to walk away.

"Yes, I do," Alexander said as he put his hand out to stop me, a solemn look on his face. We stared at one another for a moment as he dropped his hand and I stood still.

"Well," I responded. "I'll tell you tomorrow then."

He raised one eye at me in skepticism. "What, are you going to call me from Lake Como and fill me in?" I had told him earlier I would be leaving for Italy tomorrow; I had forgotten.

"Here," he said, leaning forward and gesturing for me to give him my cup. I reluctantly did so, and he poured it half full again and topped off his; I drank faster, I supposed. "Please, keep going," he said to me. He had me cornered, and I had to finish what I started.

"Alright," I responded as I walked back and sat on the couch once more, returning to the events of two days prior back home.

After getting stuck in the rain and nearly hit by a bus, I was finally back in my apartment. I went into my bathroom and quickly changed, leaving a trail of water on the floor. Back in my living room, I poured myself another drink to calm my nerves. I noticed the beautiful pink coral necklace on the coffee table that belonged to her, something we had picked up on a trip to Venice the previous summer. Uninvited, she came to my mind again. I missed her, Anastasya, alone in this austere apartment in this cold and impersonal city.

Closing my eyes as a tear escaped, I wondered how things had gotten so bad and broken. Nothing happens overnight, and this crisis had been building up for many years. It had begun fomenting in my childhood, in fact, from my earliest memories of violence, abuse in the camps, fleeing from our homeland, poverty, immigration, and resettlement in a new country. My father always said that I was weak and wouldn't amount to anything. Perhaps he was right. How many of us can reach the top in this heartless, callous, and brutally competitive 'brave new world'? Why did this matter to me anyhow; he was a monster. Why do we need validation from others?

Slamming my fist against a wall and yelling an expletive in frustration, I was too numb to feel any pain. I forced myself away from where I was and reached for my phone. That great connector, the equivalent of today's Oracle of Delphi. I secretly hoped for a message from her. I hoped for something to appear on the screen that would bring me some relief at this juncture. Looking down at this device, its bright light casting a glow on my face, there was nothing from her at all. I sighed in despair and longing. I loathed this device and wished I could smash it against a wall. I threw it down on the couch instead. We can't live without them after all.

I found myself inebriated not long after I had poured my first drink. I longed for her and grieved for him, but life has little in the way of sympathy for those caught in its relentless path. Was this my life's work and finale, I pondered now? Someone had once told me that life and the universe were indifferent to us. I felt that was accurate as I walked towards the balcony, opening the sliding door and stumbling out and facing the glorious city of structures and lights from the 30th floor. This urban heaven is reputed to be humanity's greatest good and achievement hitherto. Could that be? Is this our pinnacle, I wondered? Just then, the sharp wind cut through me and forced me to focus and stand firmer as my body teetered a bit. I kept my eyes focused on this great beast that houses so many in such little space, like a honeycomb and us the honeybees. Recalling the wisdom of Thoreau and Rousseau at this very moment, my soul hearkening back to our species' original home and hearth, the wild, I felt as though I no longer wished to be a part of this great machine.

Stepping forward, I placed my arms on the balcony ledge, my gaze growing more piercing like an eagle before it departs off a cliff. Looking down at the ground below me ominously, a dark thought came over me at just this instant. "You could be done with this very quickly, Moshe," I heard my inner voice speak to me. "One move and the pain and meaningless void could finally be quelled once and for all."

Perhaps it was true, and really, who would miss me? Would I miss life? Continuing to stare down at the ground below, the rain continued from above without mercy, drenching me for the second time this night. Thunder roared once more and pervaded the whole of the city and shook my soul with it. Though suicide is no small feat, being drunk can make it easier.

I clenched the balcony even tighter, closing my eyes and exhaling sharply. I placed my right leg over the balcony ledge as I gently pushed myself up on it as if mounting a horse. Sitting most precariously on this metallic surface that separated me from certain death below, I actually felt existence viscerally, adrenaline pumping through my veins, the taste of life and death on the tip of my tongue like blood from a rare cut of meat. My heart was pounding, my breathing rapid, my eyes wide open. All my senses were heightened. I began to cry while a numbness and paralysis set in.

"What the hell are you doing?" I managed to say to myself finally, "Get off this ledge right now, you fool."

Petrified, soaked, and unable to move, I looked down below me at just the instant that a gust of wind nudged me slightly forward, nearly knocking me over and into oblivion. My instinct to live kicked in immediately, forcing the side of my body that was hanging on the balcony to contract tightly and bring me down on the rail on my chest. Pulling myself onto the balcony with all my mortal strength, I fell heavily on my back with a thud.

In a state of utter shock and confusion, I curled up in the fetal position beside the wet wall of my apartment, trying to catch my breath. Had I actually just done that? What the hell is wrong with me, I thought at this moment? What about my family? Not a religious man, I think I prayed at that moment for the first time in many years, after which I managed to crawl back inside my apartment, rolled up on my couch, and passed out. Never had death felt so close to me.

By now, Alexander's face had changed from intent listener to aghast and worried friend. We stared at one another for a moment. I dropped my eyes off his finally. I felt embarrassed and couldn't stare at him any longer.

"Sorry," I said to him next, without emotion, my head sunk low. "This is why I didn't want you to know."

Alexander sipped the remainder of his scotch and sat back in his chair. He was actually speechless for a moment.

"Do you have a cigarette?" he finally asked me.

I was caught off guard by it, as he didn't smoke, at least not often. "Yeah, sure." I got up and retrieved my pack from my bag, and we both lit one. He got up and opened the main window.

"Listen," he said to me, "I'm not here to judge you, but I don't think you are fit to travel alone." I ashed my cigarette and looked at him, but said nothing. "Why don't you wait until the weekend and I'll come to Lake Como with you."

I laughed lightly.

"I'm not kidding, mate," he said, more seriously. I took a drag of my cigarette and looked at him as he dragged his in a funny manner befitting a non-smoker.

"Look, Alexander," I said to him, "I appreciate the concern, and I know this is all worrisome for you, but I'll be fine, you know that."

"Do you know what you just told me?" he exclaimed with a shock on his face. "That isn't a joke, you could have killed yourself!"

He was right, I could have.

"You're right, but I didn't, and that is why I'm not going back home just now."

He didn't seem convinced.

"Listen, I can take Monday off and we can go for three days and…" at which point, I abruptly interrupted him.

"No, damn it."

We both stood still and silent.

"Look, I know you're just being a friend, and I appreciate it, but I'll be fine," I said to him. "You have to trust me Alexander. Please." I wasn't a kid after all. What could he do?

He put out his cigarette and asked me to continue. I did not want to, but he made me feel guilty, saying that I owed him this at least. I obliged out of courtesy for this good friend and continued with the rest of the story.

Prying my eyes open to a sunny day, I felt incredibly groggy. I woke on the couch with my wet clothes still clinging to my cold flesh like saran wrap to a leftovers.

"What the hell?" I uttered to myself in confusion, grabbing my shirt. Sitting up, I juggled my thoughts and quickly recalled why they were wet. My heart sank as I recalled what I had attempted the night before. Anxiety reared its ugly head yet again. A piercing headache was ripping through my head. I shuddered at just how reckless I had been. Running my hands through my face, I walked over and grabbed my cigarettes. As I did, I caught a glimpse of a small, white envelope on the coffee table on top of the folders I had received the night before. Was this there the previous night? I didn't recall it.

Fighting off dizziness, I walked over and picked it up. Staring at it, I ripped it open and pulled out a small, white, folded piece of paper. Unfolding it gently, it contained four simple words: "Pursue for the truth."

Dumbfounded, I looked around the apartment and said "Hello?" I wondered if anyone else was there. That couldn't be possible. Anastasya was the only other person who had a key, and she was in London.

"Hello?" I said again, louder, looking around once more. No response. I walked towards to the door and it was locked. What the hell is going on here, I thought? Who left this for me? Tempted to open up the folders, I simply could not. I decided instead to call my sister Simona. I needed to speak with someone after last night's events.

Me and Simona were close in a cat and mouse kind of way. We loved each other, but were also always at each other's throats. She was my oldest sister, the first born, the unlucky one, you could say. Survival for her meant developing a prickly demeanour. Like myself, Simona also had many unresolved issues stemming from her childhood and the abuse she suffered at my father's hands.

Almost wary about calling her, given my fragile state and her tough love personality, I realized I had no choice. My other siblings, were not suitable for this talk. Simona was petite, but ferocious, with long, thick, dark brown hair. Her striking, exotic look was accentuated by her arched eyebrows. She was all parts beautiful and charming, but had a sharp manner about her not many could handle easily, not even my family.

I picked up my phone and called her. She picked up several rings in.

"Hey, sis, it's me."

"It's about time. Where the hell have you been? I've been calling you."

"Sorry," I responded, "I was in no mood to talk last night. Can we do lunch?"

Silence followed.

"Please, sis," I said, "I need to talk to someone. I'm not doing so well."

"Why aren't you feeling well? How long are you going to go about in pity for yourself? That asshole is gone, and frankly, it's good that she left also. It'll save you the trouble later."

I placed the phone on my chest, wishing she would desist from such talk, but I continued talking.

"Simona, please, I can't handle this right now. Can you just meet me for lunch?"

"Jesus, relax, you say it like I have a choice. I don't want mom having to endure more shit because of any of us, and its time you started doing your part and reducing her worries."

What could I say to her?

"Meet me at Spencer's on the waterfront near your place in an hour for lunch. I don't have much time, so don't be late." I hated Spencer's, but reluctantly agreed. "Do me a favour before and call mom," she said to me before going. "She is quite worried about you, as if she doesn't have enough to worry about."

"Alright," I lied, "I will."

I was in no state to talk with my mother. I got off the phone with her, showered quickly, changed, and headed over to the restaurant, leaving the folders and the note behind.

Late as usual, Simona finally arrived, on the phone speaking expressively with someone, barely looking at me before she sat down. Ending the call a minute later, she looked at me with an inquisitive and unforgiving look.

"So, what's up?" she said. "What's wrong with you now?"

I was used to such harsh treatment from her. Unable to lie, I took a deep breath and told her everything. I couldn't lie to her; she knew me too well. She was quite shocked by everything, as evidenced by the number of times she would say "Oh, my God." I'm not even sure if she believed in God, quite frankly.

"Seriously, what the hell is wrong with you? Do you want to kill mother and hurt us all too? Are you that selfish?" Harsh as it was, she was right. "Perhaps you need more medication," she said as she checked her phone. I hated when people did that during a conversation.

"I'm thinking of going to London to get her back," I told her, coyly and quickly to get her attention. She raised her head up, brows lifted in dismay.

"You must be insane! She is not the answer, nor the solution. You are just vulnerable right now and you want comfort," she yelled at me. Embarrassed, I look around to see if anyone was watching us; they weren't.

"You need help, brother. You are the source of your problems with women. How many times has this happened in the last few years? You need to deal with your issues once and for all. No woman will put up with your lying, cheating, and manipulating ways forever you know, no matter how much they love you."

I dropped my eyes down on the table as I played with my glass. She was right. I had cheated and manipulated Anastasya on several occasions. I didn't have much to say. We sat there quietly for a few more minutes until she got a call and got up to leave.

"I've got a busy day, and I think you need to think things over." I said nothing, but looked up at her. "Stay put. Don't go anywhere," were her final words. I merely nodded my head as she walked away.

What could I say after all? She was probably right. How long could I continue on with my ways? Was I a product of the liberal times we lived in, where short-term pleasure and gain was the prevalent manner of living, whether in one's vocation or in one's romantic endeavours? I felt as though society shapes us like clay, paints us in the wrong colours, and finally shatters us into pieces. This is no way to live. Eventually, we must all wake up.

On the walk home, I called my mother. We had a comfortable conversation with the usual pleasantries and words of love and comfort on her part. Although she had been separated from my father for many years, I knew this was still tough for her, so naturally, I kept her out of my problems. She had endured enough in life, and we were always protective of her. I did, however, briefly mention the envelopes that belonged to my father that I received the previous night, hoping she might know something about them. She claimed she did not, but something about her response seemed puzzling to me. Her tone had seemed to change abruptly when I brought them up, almost as if she was caught off guard. This made me even more curious as to their contents. Regardless, I was glad I finally managed to call mother; hearing her voice always calmed my spirits. I promised her I would visit as soon as possible.

The apartment felt stale. I opened a window to let in some fresh air. What was I going to do with myself? I was actually afraid to be alone after last night. Judging by Simona, my family would clearly not support me pursuing her; that much was obvious now. What did they know about me and her relationship anyways, I thought to myself, dismissing them in frustration. Then again, maybe they were right. Maybe she wasn't the right person for me, or maybe I wasn't ready for her, or anyone for that matter?

My anxiety began to resurface at thinking these thoughts. I noticed the envelopes on the coffee table again, which drew my attention. What the hell was in them anyways? I began walking towards them, but was interrupted by a call. To my surprise, it was Michelle. She was a longtime fling who lived in Montreal. She was 25 or 26, I couldn't remember. Tall, dark, an aspiring actress, she was fun, but vivacious and well, somewhat twisted and depraved. I had met her during an event I had hosted in Montreal a few years back, and we've had a relationship of sorts ever since.

I sat down, distracted, rubbing my head, wondering if I should call her back. I succumbed and I did. Apparently, she was in town for the weekend and wanted to meet up. I knew what would come of the rendezvous. A part of me welcomed the distraction, but the other realized it contradicted my whole pursuit of Anastasya, and I felt torn, pacing around the room in deliberation. We are what we are, I suppose. Temptation tempted and I could not resist; I was weak. She would be over by 9 p.m.

It was well past midnight, and several empty bottles of wine were strewn about us as we lay on the couch in my living room, lights dimmed, candle burning. Michelle had removed her top and my shirt. She was staring up at me, her eyes tinted with lust, her delicate skin radiating a youthful glow. She had an amorous smirk on her face. Reaching under my jeans with her left hand, she used the other to undo the first two buttons. It all felt wrong.

"Michelle," I said to her as I grabbed her hand.

"Just relax," she replied. I dropped my head back on the couch, staring up at the ceiling, exhaling. Feeling a few more buttons undone, I lifted my head again and restrained her other hand as well.

"Michelle, please," I said. Her smile faded a bit, but still had the squint of the devil in it. Both hands restrained, she seemed to relish her confinement and began to press her lips on my navel, caressing my stomach with her tongue, staring up at me. I felt aroused, but guilty, finally forcing myself up and yelling "Stop it, already."

She was startled. So was I, frankly. I wasn't in the habit of turning down beautiful women. She stood up, her expression completely changed.

"What the hell is wrong you?" she yelled at me. "Why are you acting this way? You invited me over, remember!" I had indeed, she was right. "I don't need this shit, I've got plenty of options, you know," she yelled, turning around. I grabbed her by the wrist then as she attempted to walk away. "Let go of me, right now," she yelled.

"Or what?" I said back to her defiantly. She attempted to jerk herself free once more, and this time, I pulled her right back into me. She was the type of girl that loved being baited in such ways. I was the type of guy who hated hearing that I wasn't the only option. I pulled her closer and placed my hand around her back, while the other cupped her face. My thumb pressed on her lips, pulling on it gently. It was the perfect situation really. Most women suffer from wanting to be dominated. Most men suffer more from wanting to dominate. It was an acute display of the sordid underbelly of what makes our species tick, and for the first time in the last few weeks, I felt vigorous and alive again.

Reaching behind her head, I grabbed her thick, black hair and tugged on it, pulling her head back and exposing her neck, making her gasp. I had her, all of her. The neckline is the no man's land between body and mind. Past the point of no return, I threw her on the couch and pulled off her garments. For a brief period of time, all my problems and worries seemed to vanish.

I woke on the couch the next morning feeling rather groggy and hungover. I turned over to see a dark, long haired figure beside me asleep, which startled me. I quickly recalled who it was: Michelle. Naturally, she had stayed over and we had slept together, true to form for me. I felt rather lowly about myself recalling parts of the night. Maybe my sister was right. Perhaps I needed to face myself and my personal issues once and for all. Here I was, a broken man full of repressed, unresolved traumas, dealing with losses and looking for solutions in all the wrong places. I was also looking for a solution to a modern life that no longer enchanted me, yet had bound me to it like it does so many others.

I dropped my head in despair, running my hands through my hair as I asked the universe for a sign, for some direction or guidance. I got up and made my way outside and onto the balcony to countenance a beautiful, sunny day, the same balcony that yesterday had been my nightmare. Standing there, a calm day, I closed my eyes. They were opened a moment later when I heard the delightful sound of a flock of birds. I turned around to behold a beautiful sight, a dozen or so of these graceful creatures flying together in formation. My heart fluttered out of beat for a minute as I looked upon them. I longed to be just like these birds at that instant, wishing I had wings that I could stretch and use to fly up and away as well. I was transfixed on these magnificent guardians of the sky as if nothing else in the world existed.

As they flew further away and out of sight, I had a profound epiphany and realization. I too would fly away and chase the horizon like these majestic animals. I would go to London to get her back. Never had I looked at the sky, the sun, or the horizon as I did this morning. It was as if I was looking at these things for the first time with a brand new set of eyes. Something happened within me then and there.

When I finally finished telling Alexander everything, I couldn't quite believe it all myself. He said nothing for a moment. Neither did

I. I looked at my watch and noticed it was past 2 a.m.

"Well," I said, then paused.

"Well, what?" he responded.

"You asked me what led me here, and I told you."

He just stared at me, then finally shook his head and stood up.

"What's wrong?" I asked him.

He stepped forward, put his hands on my shoulders, and looked me straight in the eyes. "You asked for a sign, and it seems you got it." I wasn't sure what he meant by that, so I nodded. "Just don't waste it," he said to me.

"Waste what?" I asked him.

"The chance to become a better person." He lifted his arms off me, a bit inebriated perhaps, as they swung a bit and his eyes rolled. "I worry about you, you know that, you crazy son of a bitch."

I chuckled at him. "No need to. I'll be fine, I promise."

He turned around, walked away, and said, "you should worry about yourself sometimes, and the people that love you."

That one stung a bit more. It made me think of her just then, sending an arrow through my heart. I wasn't as good to her as she was to me, Anastasya. I knew that.

"And don't you leave without saying bye in the morning," he yelled loudly, out of view and down the hall, his door closing shut right after with a loud thud. A true friend, Alexander.

I stood still for a moment, then finally poured myself a nightcap, turned off the light, and sat on the couch, staring out the window and thinking about everything in the dark. Eventually, I fell asleep.

Chapter 3:
The Dream

To get to Lake Como, I first had to go to Milan. From there, it was an hour-long train ride. The trip to Milan was relatively straightforward and quick. It was early evening as the airport express was pulling into the central station, creaking as it did, revealing its age. This station was a work of art. Looking up while walking past the gates, great, large Roman arches lined the main pavilion. Looking down a moment later, I was walking on black and white marble that shined and glistened.

My train pulled in not long after, and the doors opened with the loud noise of compressed air being released from underneath the carriage. It was one of those days when it felt as though the world was working along with you and everything arrived just when you did. Boarding, I sat at a window seat, perhaps a tinge of excitement overcoming me, gazing outside my window. Fully boarded, the doors closed, and we began pulling out of the station. It was all like a postcard, or an old movie, except she never came running after the train.

The short trip was pleasant, with fresh views of the Italian countryside and all its summer splendour. Nature resonates with our souls more than anything else in life. We are, after all, its greatest offspring. About an hour later, we entered Como Lago Nord station, a miniscule one compared to Milan's. A short while later, I was standing outside the township of Como, just as the sun was setting on this beautiful and romantic place. Walking towards my hotel with the guide of a local map, I couldn't help but feel lighter here than I had in London. Perhaps it was the water, or simply the fact that I could actually hear and see nature here and not just civilization.

The hotel was rather small. I checked in and walked up to the third floor to my room, a small, but quaint little apartment, warm, with ample daylight and old wood floors. Opening the tall, double balcony windows, I stepped outside. I could see the marina and the lake, as well as the outlines of the tall valleys, peaks, and far-off mountains, some of them with snow on their summits. It was indeed quite a charming and sublime landscape, so very different from the city. I inhaled deeply, and for the first time in many days, hope visited my heart.

Waking up to a bright, sunny day the next morning, I felt a strange feeling of joy and confusion. It normally happens when you're away from home in a foreign place. You don't recognize where you are at first, but once you do, you're happy you aren't at home. Stretching my arms, sitting upright on my bed, I felt a bit torn about being here. I wasn't sure where I should be anymore. Feeling homeless, I shook my head and reaffirmed to myself why I had come here instead of going home: I needed solitude to figure things out. I needed a break from my life, from the city. It would also give me a chance to peruse through my father's folders in peace and quiet and perhaps get to know the man a bit more posthumously.

Back inside, I placed my right hand in my black travel bag. I felt around for them, but couldn't feel them or see them and began to panic. "Oh, my God," I said. "Where are they?" Grabbing the bag and furiously shaking its contents onto the bed, my heart sank like a ship's anchor as they were nowhere in sight. "Please, no, where the hell are they?" Frantic, I looked all over the room, even dropping on my knees to look under the bed. I looked everywhere, but found nothing.

Seated at the edge of my bed, my hands clasped my face in frustration. It dawned upon me finally: I left them on the train. I had taken them out once the train had rolled out of the station in Milan, but was shortly thereafter interrupted by the train officer who had asked me for my ticket. I put everything back in the folders and placed them to my side between the seat and the wall of the carriage at that point to attend to him, forgetting about them afterwards.

Sprinting across the township of Como, I narrowly missed a few pedestrians along the way, drawing a few responses in Italian, local expletives I'm sure. Arriving at the train station out of breath, I realized I had to stop smoking. An old Italian man stood staring at me blankly. I nodded at him, but he simply continued to stare at me. I made my way in and ran to the first counter I saw that was open.

"Hello, excuse me." The attendant, a middle-aged man, raised his brows to acknowledge me. "I have an emergency," I shouted at him across the glass.

"Yes, sir," he responded.

"Yesterday, I rode the train into Como, but I left some very important documents beside my seat. Please, I need you to help me and see if anyone has returned them. They are very important to me."

Seeming unsure as to what to do, he calmly asked me to wait a moment as he left to speak with someone else. Unable to stand still, I paced back and forth for a few moments. The attendant finally reappeared with another individual, a younger man.

"Yes, sir," he said to me with a smile, "I understand you have lost something on the train yesterday?"

"Yes, yes, some legal documents in an orange folder, they are very important," I said, flustered.

"Of course," he said to me. "Do you remember what time the train arrived in Como?"

I closed my eyes, squinting, trying to remember. "7:30 p.m. or so. Yes, around this time," I said to him, leaning forward on the counter.

"Okay. Unfortunately, we have nothing here with us. No one dropped anything off from the train last night, but I will call Milan station to see if it was recovered there perhaps."

Livid with myself for even being in this situation, I kicked the wall below the window, startling both men.

"I'm sorry," I said, both of them looking at me askance. "Please, can you call and find out, I cannot rest until I have them."

The younger man nodded and promised that he would, asking me to take a seat in the meanwhile. He seemed genuine and honest, but then again, so do many people before you get to know them. Not all, but many.

It had been 10 minutes and I was growing tired of waiting, so I returned to the counter.

"Hello. Any news?" I said to the older man again, who looked at me blankly and motioned for me to walk around to the side and knock on the door. I did, knocking rather hard and eliciting a response on the other side in Italian, again probably expletives. It seemed that I was spreading cheer in Italy.

The young man opened the door, smiling, and said, "Yes, sir, you are lucky!"

If you only knew, I thought to myself, as my face lit up at his words.

"The cleaners recovered your folders at the end of the night shift while cleaning the carriage and turned it in; however, it is at Milan Station."

A sigh of relief followed. "Thank you, thank you so much," I said. He advised me that they would be delivered on the next train to Como.

"Is it safe? Will it arrive for sure?" I said to him. He laughed. "Yes, of course it will arrive. I give you my word." What choice did I have?

"Alright," I said. "When will it arrive?"

Rolling his eyebrows, he shrugged his shoulder, gesturing that he did not know. "Give me your number and we will call you when it is here, perhaps in a few hours, sir."

Writing it down on a piece of paper for him, I thanked him and his staff and made my way back to the hotel. Relieved and breathing normally again, I had just evaded disaster. I was grateful to the soul that turned them in. You just never know in life. The smallest act can mean the world to another. There is still good amongst us; all is not lost. Realizing how easy it might have been for them to be thrown away or go missing, I now felt as though I was destined to know what was in these folders and whatever they contained about my father, family, or history. It is indeed true what they say, that although the truth may travel a thousand miles and visit a hundred places, it will always find its way home.

As I stepped out of the station, I found myself nervous and at a loss about where I was and what I was doing. Looking across the street randomly towards the piazza, I thought I saw her, Anastasya. I became jittery, pacing forward a few steps to look more closely at this figure that very much resembled her. Yes, it was her, I was sure. My eyes flung open in excitement and surprise as I hopped onto the street, just avoiding a scooter and then receiving a loud honk from a truck that whizzed just past me. Unable to restrain my legs, I sprinted forward and ran across the street towards where she was, near a cathedral. As I moved quickly through the crowd and towards the door, finally reaching her, I grabbed her on the right shoulder, utterly startling her as she turned around. My jaw dropped and my mouth froze open, on the cusp of uttering something. It wasn't her after all. This young woman stared at me in shock.

"I'm so sorry," I said out. "I thought you were someone else. Please forgive me."

She seemed displeased; I had grabbed her after all. Embarrassed, I stepped aside as people looked on and she turned around and walked in. What the hell is wrong with you? I thought to myself.

I heard music emanate from the church and looked up to notice its beautiful façade, a large circular dome at its top and statues of saints on its side. I had nothing else to do anyhow but wait. I made my way in with the crowd. It was dark inside, with small candles lit everywhere and a walkway that led to the pews and seating section. A young father caught me staring at him just then and gestured for me to enter and take a seat. I felt uncomfortable and walked to the right instead with jittery movements. Around the corner, I stood beside a pillar as the choir and pipes echoed through this beautiful and old building of faith. I am not a religious man, but a house of God is a house of God regardless of where you are. I enjoyed hearing the melody and sound echo throughout this place as many sat down, kneeled, and did the cross in supplication.

I closed my eyes for a moment, feeling a temporary peace, but it was quickly interrupted by someone.

"Why don't you take a seat, my son?"

I opened my eyes to see the father who had greeted me just a moment ago standing beside me. He was small, but amiable looking, a smile on his face and hand across his chest, holding the holy book.

"No, thank you, father, I'm fine." He continued staring at me. I felt awkward. "I'd like to be alone if that's alright." I said.

"Certainly," he responded. "However, may I speak something to you from the heart?" I nodded. "Let it go and move forward with God."

What the hell did that mean? "Let what go, father?" I said, squinting at him.

"Let them go, they are one with the past now."

I relaxed my shoulder from the pillar and stepped off a bit. I felt uncomfortable and suspicious of this person in front of me.

"Become like a child again, start over," he whispered to me as I retreated. The crescendo of the pipes startled me just then, and I finally turned around and made my way out in haste, the haunting and hollow music echoing all around me as I fled.

Outside, my heart was racing, and I felt uneasy about everything, including where I was. I needed a drink. There were many sidewalk bars with chairs and tables in the square. I made my way to the one on the far right corner with the least people, sat down, had a cigarette, and ordered a beer. I had to keep it together. I was starting to see things and people that weren't there and that is never a good sign. Why did he say "leave them behind," the father? How did he know? What the hell did "become like a child" mean anyways? My beer arrived just then, and I drank it quickly and ordered another.

It was almost an hour and four pints later before I finally got the call from the train station. Arriving at the station, I was short of breath, having sprinted there anxious to have the documents back in my possession. An immense relief came over me upon receiving them. Thanking the kind staff who had helped me, I made my way back to the hotel. I had essentially squandered a whole day and not really cared that I had. Sometimes there is nothing more worthwhile or life-affirming than simply killing time doing nothing.

I opened a bottle of wine, grabbed the notebook I was looking at yesterday, and started at the beginning. The passages were not in any particular order, nor were they all dated. My father was a dense writer. I came upon one particular passage that had a title that captured my attention: "Washington DC – 1994".

I remembered it faintly at first, but then quite well. When we first arrived in Canada, my father, I'm sure longing for his former life, had continued to remain engaged where possible with things back home in Iran. Many in the Iranian diaspora, who were staunchly against the prevailing regime, tried to exert pressure through engagement with foreign governments such as the U.S. Washington was home to one of the largest annual marches, where a multitude of Iranian groups converged to show a unified voice against a repressive, authoritarian, and corrupt regime back home. My family had never returned to Iran after we fled in 1987. In fact, we were not allowed to do so by the Canadian government for our own safety of course.

Thinking of my father, holding his files, my eyes welled up. He was lucky to have escaped prison with his life intact. Sadly, the same could not be said of his body. He endured extensive torture during his imprisonment in Tehran, causing irreparable physical and mental damage. We were lucky to have been able to flee the country at that time. I'd like to think destiny had played a hand in it. Neither of my parents had ever attempted to return home, not even for a visit. Neither could they afford to do so frankly. Though we may forget it nowadays, especially the younger generation, travel is a luxury, not a right. The world wasn't nearly as accessible as it is today just a decade ago even.

My father had never worked after we left Iran. Prison had left him partially disabled and suffering from severe post-traumatic stress disorder. My mother had always been a housewife. She singlehandedly raised all six children under the harshest of conditions. I always found it ironic that my father managed to get us out of Iran, away from tyranny and abuse, only to subject us to both all our lives inside our own home.

I continued perusing this passage, taking another sip of my drink which had become warm. I went on this trip with my father, the only one we ever took together. My mother did not approve of me going.

Politically charged rallies were, after all, hardly a place for a 12-year-old to be at. She had tried to stop my father, for which she received a vicious beating. Recalling her face after that episode gave me shivers. Traumas of life are seared into our psyches like tattoos on our skin, and we can never forget them. They will forever be there, somewhere.

Upset, distraught by the details returning to me, I shut the notebook and pounded it on the bed, uttering profanity at life and at my father. This only made me feel worse, because it is wrong to insult the dead. Picking up the notebook again, I hurled it against the wall and headed onto the balcony, hoping that the fresh air would assuage my agony. I was shivering like a child in the dark. Perhaps I should just stop right now with all of this and return home, but I couldn't. I had been running from this most of my life. Like so many others, just running from my past. I had a window of opportunity to confront it once and for all. I could not resist it as windows into the past provide something we desire and another which we are drawn to: hindsight and nostalgia.

Peering out the window, I was startled by several loud knocks on my door now. Turning around, I froze, wondering who it could be.

"Hello?" No response. "Hello?" Nothing. I tepidly walked over and stood behind the door, placing my hand on the knob, but unsure as to whether I should open it or not. I finally pulled it open, to my surprise, seeing no one in sight.

"Hello?" I said again, my voice echoing down the stairs. Who could it have been, I knew no one here? Perhaps the owner, but why would he knock and leave? It was all rather strange. I went inside and called the front desk to inquire, but they were as stumped as I was. "that's odd" I quietly whispered.

Noticing the notebook on the floor, I picked it up and began to look over a few more obscure passages, including one recounting an incident of torture while in prison that led to damage in my father's right eye and ear. His description was disturbing and grotesque. He would lose function in both later in life. A true writer, his words were heavy; the truth often is.

Drained from reading, I decided to look over some of his pictures instead. There was quite a large stack of them, many of my family and few of which I had never seen. Mother was a truly beautiful woman; I could see why my father pursued her so vigorously. Sadly, in all these pictures, you could always see hints of misery in her eyes. She seldom wore a smile and always stood rigid and still, as if in fear. She likely was, the poor thing. I missed her terribly. She was a woman living in a prison with her husband as both a cellmate and a guard. In fact, the whole family lived in this cell.

The next picture caught my attention, as it contained a young girl who appeared in several other pictures. This time, however, she was in the hands of an older woman wearing a headscarf. Who was this person, I thought to myself, turning it around to reveal a word on the back: "Kurdistan." The word immediately conjured old memories of a place I had visited as a young boy. Kurdistan was a semi-autonomous region that spanned several countries in the Middle East and was defined by an ethnic group, that much like the Jews or Armenians, had always been persecuted and had no clearly defined homeland. I recalled that my father would often travel there clandestinely to do work with a banned communist party he was a member of. Flipping the picture back around, my eyes and thoughts returned to this woman. Who could she be, and why did he have these pictures of her and this young girl?

There was a magazine at the bottom of the folder that drew my attention. It contained a particularly striking image on the cover. A naked man shown from his side, hung upside down from chains on his legs, which were tied up against a hauntingly thick hook and black back drop. I opened the magazine to a creased page that contained a picture I quickly recognized. It was my family, at the time without my two younger brothers, who had not yet been born. The picture was part of an article about my family and my father, I inferred. I did not know what it meant, as I could not read Turkish, but the picture on the next page was unmistakable: it was a picture of the camp we had stayed at in Istanbul.

Immediately dropping the magazines from my hands, I retreated back quickly, coming hard upon the wall with my back. The memories this picture evoked left me aghast, my face drawn open with an expression of horror as if I had witnessed a ghost. A hard enough experience on its own, I had personally endured an ordeal there that was immensely traumatic and continued to haunt me to this day. I had never dealt with it, I simply couldn't; it was too painful. Enough for one night. I forced myself asleep.

I woke up startled and breathing rapidly. I snapped out of bed as if I was having a seizure, legs and arms swinging wildly. It was only just a nightmare. Sitting up, I began to regain my composure and felt some relief, breathing more regularly. I recalled the dream vividly nonetheless, despite wanting to forget about it. Walking over to the balcony, I stepped out into another beautiful summer day in paradise. Not even the sun could assuage my heart. What the hell did this dream mean? Dreams are, after all, a conversation between the conscious and subconscious mind; they mean something. They are gateways.

This one was a particularly vivid dream. A small, dark, square room. On the left, there was an opaque mirror window. In the centre, a bed you'd find in a psychoanalyst's office and me situated on it, lying down ominously. There was a large painting in front of me. Thinking upon it, it was of the Blue Mosque in Istanbul. The room had an otherwise hazy, grey colour to it and felt tight and constrictive. The next thing I noticed was a couple to my left. It could have been any couple, dressed normal in plain clothes. Something in particular stuck out about them however. They had no faces. No visible features whatsoever, just a blurry outline of a short man and woman. I could hear them as well, and what they said was eerie: "We only buried his body, not his soul. He is still here, he hasn't left."

My heart was palpitating by this point. I couldn't move my body. Looking down and to my front again, just below the picture, there was a young child. He was sitting on the floor, an empty look on his face, no expression whatsoever. Peering more closely, I was stunned. It was me when I was a child.

What happened next finally woke me. The young child slowly lifted his gaze away from mine and looked slightly up and to his right. He was looking at someone behind me. Petrified, I wasn't even sure I wanted to know who it was. Twisting my neck with effort as my body was stiff, I turned around to see a figure slowly emerge from behind a small wall. It was my father. I wasn't sure at first. His face was wearied, more wrinkled than I recalled, his skin tanned. He was also much shorter than he was in person. My heart was racing by now, as I had not yet seen him in my dreams since he passed away. Before I woke, he smiled at me. My father never smiled at me in life. As quickly as he appeared, he began to drift back behind the wall, fading out of sight, smiling as he did. He seemed to be at peace.

The dream had shaken me. Sometimes dreams are so vivid, we are left wondering whether we are in fact awake or still dreaming upon coming to from them. Sometimes they leave us feeling hopeful, beautiful. Other times they leave us feeling dreadful. Such is their power. We forget sometimes that we create the dreams we have. They say something about us. We are, after all, their architects.

There was only one person who could decipher and make sense of dreams in my life, my mother. I had to call her.

"Moshe, my boy!" Spending a few moments on the usual pleasantries, I got to it. I asked her what the dream meant. "My son, I beg you, stop looking into the past. Move forward already."

I listened respectfully. Forward? Forward where, I thought?

"Are you there?" she said. "Yes, mom, I'm here." She was an incredibly strong woman, but also fragile. She had lived a hard life. I had to be cautious. Deferring questions about the documents, the pictures, I was growing frustrated, but kept calm. Our generation lacks patience. We no longer see eye to eye with our parents because we no longer see or live in the same world as them. Life moves and changes so fast these days that it is nearly impossible to grasp. Is it not?

"How about Turkey, mom, the camps, Istanbul?" I asked her. My mother was the only person in the world who knew about the horrible experience I personally endured in Istanbul.

"You already know everything about that." The phone went silent. "I love you, Moshe," she said to me. "You are much better than him and you have a different future before you. Please, I beg you, leave it and move on."

I wasn't going to press her any more, she didn't deserve it. "Yes, mother. You're right," I said to satisfy her. Some lies are justified. We bid each other a heartfelt goodbye.

Early afternoon, I walked along the waterside, gathering my thoughts and trying to absorb some of the beauty of this place. Small details, like the pattern in which the moss was growing against the rocks, they stood out to me. The hillsides were lush and green, canopies of foliage interspersed with beautiful, old villas and homes. The air here seemed purer. Sometimes when we get lost in nature, we catch a real glimpse of life, of our higher selves. Earth, air, fire, water; all life is this, elements. The rest is just concepts and distractions, but as beautiful as Lake Como was, the dream of my fortnight was a distraction that wouldn't relent from my mind.

I recalled something else, something that took place in Istanbul where we lived in the camps. Perhaps that was the message in all of this: Istanbul. Perhaps it was time to go back to this place of my past where something seminal had happened to me. Something terrible that I had never addressed, but had always affected me. Maybe that was the whole purpose of the dream, to force me to finally address this dark stain on my life once and for all. Why did my father appear in it however?

Luckily, I had family in Istanbul. Uncle Ammad lived there with his wife and two children. He wasn't an actual blood uncle, I merely called him that because I had known him since childhood, since Turkey, in fact. It had been at least three years since I last saw him and his family. He did not make it to my father's funeral because of an illness in his immediate family in Iran; otherwise, he would most certainly have flown over for the ceremony. He was principled like that. For whatever reason, he was quite fond of my father. I guess things are different to those on the outside than those on the inside.

I called him up immediately and was quite relieved when his wife, Gelareh, whom I referred to as aunt for the same reason, picked up. It seemed my uncle was busy with work. I told her that I would be coming to Istanbul for a visit and would need a place to stay. Naturally, she was delighted and welcomed me with open arms. I had been to Istanbul only once since my childhood and that was in transit. This would be a more meaningful trip. I hoped to find out more about my father and finally take a stand against my past and confront it. When you're at rock bottom, there's nowhere else to go but up. What did I have to lose anymore? What did I care about consequences? What had caring about various things all these years bring me? My life lacked purposed and meaning. To hell with it all.

I came to a stop on the tip of the road that punched out sharply over the edge and onto the lake. Standing still, I looked around this majestic and beautiful landscape that I had to leave so early after arriving. I wasn't ready for it yet, but I vowed that I would return one day when I was. One day when I was a better man, more whole, more at peace.

Chapter 4:
Back in Time

We hold love in the highest regard and as our greatest good, but are often too afraid to pursue it. It is, after all, the riskiest investment we will ever make. Like truth, love is often elusive, but her allure is too overwhelming to resist. I had lost love once again, but I vowed to free myself of my past.

No longer able to enjoy Lake Como, I had left and was now in Turkey, having transited through Milan the previous day. This whole trip had taken quite a detour and twist. I hadn't even told anyone about it yet, except for my uncle and aunt who were receiving me here. Putting it out of mind for now as I was walking through the large, congested terminal at Istanbul's airport, I stopped. Looking ahead and up at the all-glass façade that soaked this place in daylight, my chest heaved in and out like the tide. It was hot and muggy outside. I was looking for a blue Toyota sedan driven by my aunt Gelareh. I did not miss the city, that's for sure.

Having looked through a few more of my father's notes on the plane ride over, I had found out that he was involved politically, even here in Turkey amongst Iranian refugees. There were references to various names of officials at the camps, though I doubted any of them were still around so many years later. It was a starting point at least. I was getting anxious thinking about this all. Was I really in Istanbul pursuing such matters, given the current state of my life? My hands were trembling like cups on tables when a train passes by. I reached for my cigarettes. Aunt Gelareh was quite late, and I was starting to feel nervous about this all.

A minute later, I noticed a blue Toyota sedan approaching from afar and began walking towards it on the road, recklessly. My aunt saw me as I began to wave and started honking repeatedly, startling and embarrassing me. I made my way back onto the pedestrian side to wait for her, hoping she would stop honking and pull over. Wishful thinking on my part. I seemed to have forgotten just what a character she was. She honked all the way towards where I stood, drawing many eyes and ears. I had long stopped waving or looking over, shoulders taut, head down, hiding. Incredibly, she drove right past me, waving from inside wildly to me with a fully formed, open mouth smile, her frizzy hair completing her caricature. Several cars ahead, she parked on a complete slant, with the tail out on oncoming traffic. I watched with eyes wide open as she stepped out right there and began waddling towards me with her thick frame, like an overzealous and joyful penguin.

"Hey!" she blurted out loudly, calling my name several times while waiving her right hand in the air as if I couldn't see her, clutching her purse with her left.

"Oh, my God," I muttered to myself quietly, completely embarrassed by the whole thing.

"Hey, you handsome boy!" she said, nearing me. I smiled as she made impact with a hug, tipping on her toes to give me several kisses on the cheeks. We looked at each other for a moment, smiling. It had been three years after all. "I'm so happy to see you," she said to me.

"You don't age, Auntie," I said smiling. "It's good to see you too. Thanks for coming to get me." I felt comfortable and loved here already, if even just for the fleeting moment. Isn't that all we ever want after all?

"Hey, lady," I heard now as we both looked back at a clearly exasperated officer pointing to her car.

"Okay, okay, officer, just catching up with my nephew," she yelled back as she put her hands around my back and hugged me smiling, facing him as if he cared. Her head barely reached my shoulders. She brought such levity to any environment. Aunt Gelareh is one of those people – we all know at least one – that we look at and secretly envy or dislike because they seem genuinely happy.

It was early evening when we arrived at my aunt and uncle's home in the northern suburbs of Istanbul, a middle class, residential area. It was a nice place, a fine neighbourhood, but suburb living was too quiet, too sedentary for me. I could infer from the aroma of jasmine and saffron that she had been busy cooking earlier. My aunt was the consummate housewife and homemaker, her home adorned with childish and warm knick-knacks. Uncle Ammad was at work, but was expected home shortly alongside Nav, their son and my cousin who would now be 21 or 22. Their daughter, Dori, a few years Nav's junior, had been away this week on a trip with her gymnastics team. That was a shame.

The family ran a successful import/export business that they had started back in Canada, but had since relocated to Turkey years ago. Most of their business was in the Middle East and Asia. Uncle Ammad's mother had fallen ill in her old age. He wanted to be closer to her in case things got really bad, like they did with his father, who had died of cancer years back. He wasn't able to be there for him. He didn't want to repeat the same shortcoming with his mother.

Looking at old pictures in the living room, some containing my family and my father, I heard that unmistakable voice. "He was better looking than you, you have to admit that." Smiling, I put down the frame in my hand and turned around to see Uncle Ammad standing by the stairs, chuckling.

"Hello, young man," he said as he walked to me. "At least you still got hair." He ran his hands through my hair and chuckled again. He was a joker after all; no wonder he loved my aunt, she was a clown. Embracing him warmly, I noticed Nav now behind him. He had grown quite a bit in three years, looking more the part a man than the young boy I recalled. His arms and legs showed a lot more artwork, a passion of his that his parents were not particularly fond of, but could do nothing about. We stood there, the three of us chatting, laughing, and catching up until my aunt called us for dinner. "Let's eat," she said excitedly in her squeaky voice, clapping her hands in the air.

Medium built, partially bald, with a sparse beard and a trademark moustache, Uncle Ammad worked hard and kept life simple, and it showed. He was an academic, he liked books. Not an activist like my father, his was more of a love for knowledge than a love for justice. He wasn't a fighter.

"Hey, hey, I got one," he said, posing a joke for us. "Why did the duck run and not walk across the road?" No one responded. "It was quacker," he said, laughing at his own joke. "Get it? Quacker!" We all laughed out of courtesy. Seeing him interact with his family saddened me, reminding me that I never had such a relationship with my father. Uncle Ammad respected him tremendously. I recall him saying on many occasions that my father was responsible for his success because of the opportunity he had given him. I never quite understood what that meant, nor did I ask. What opportunity had he given Uncle Ammad? There was never any conversation in my family about my father. We avoided him in every way, wherever and whenever possible. Ironically, everyone else seemed to be in love with him or at least respected him. This always confounded me. No two people see the same person alike. Some see a saint, while others see a sinner. What was there to like about him anyways, that monster, that tyrant?

I heard my name called abruptly, drawing my head and eyes up. "You okay?" I had momentarily slipped away, it seemed.

"Yes, yes," I said, clenching my eyes shut and open. "Just tired from the trip" I lied.

"Did you want a back rub?"

"I'm sorry, a back rub?" I responded.

"Yes" my uncle said, "a back rub, you know, after your long and hard trip all the way from Italy."

I dropped my head and laughed. Uncle was an incorrigible funny man. "Your generation today, I tell you," he said as he grabbed Nav's head and rubbed his scalp in jest, "you wouldn't last a day in my time." He was probably right. We are spoiled nowadays, everything at the tip of our hands, one button away. Has such comfort and convenience made us any happier?

Finally making our way into the dining room, we all sat down before a spread worthy of a king. Nothing lifts the spirit like a home cooked meal. Afterwards, we caught up on lost time, sharing old memories and many laughs. Uncle Ammad suggested heading down to the old town near the Blue Mosque for tobacco pipe smoking and drinks. Nav was off to see his girlfriend, so he was out. Aunt Gelareh wasn't into smoking or drinking. "Oh, that thing with the bubbles and smoke," she said with a dismissive gesture of her hands in the air. "That's just silly. Silly, silly," she reiterated, walking away with some dishes.

"And you, Moshe," my uncle said to me. "Are you available or do you need your beauty sleep?" I chuckled. "Sure, I'm up for it, Uncle Ammad." Kissing my aunt and thanking her for the wonderful meal, I made my way upstairs to change.

Not long after, I was back out on the road in Istanbul for a rather scenic drive across town and alongside the Bosphorous River that separated the city in two. It was dark, giving this city of my past a mysterious and foreboding ambience. Shortly thereafter, we were in the vicinity of the Blue Mosque, the place I had seen in my dream just a fortnight ago. We parked and began to walk in an area full of tourist attractions, restaurants, and cafes.

We had been walking for a good 15-20 minutes, sharing small talk. "I want to ask you something," my uncle said, a change in his tone. "Why have you decided to come to Turkey all of a sudden?" I looked at him and he looked back at me.

"Let's sit down at a bar, Uncle Ammad." He nodded in agreement. We sat down at the next bar we crossed, an authentic Turkish one with dark wood furniture, thick cotton carpets, and an abundance of smoke from tobacco pipes. We ordered and nibbled on some dried nuts while the pipe and beers were delivered.

Uncle cut the silence. "You are like a son to me, you know that, right?" I nodded, my shallow eyes and hunched posture revealing my heaviness. "I get the feeling you aren't just her to see us, but have other business."

I couldn't respond just now; we both went quiet for a moment.

"I'm sorry about your father, I truly am," he said. I nodded in response, unable to face him. I decided to bring Uncle Ammad up to speed on my life, especially everything that had recently happened, including, of course, Anastasya. He listened faithfully, but seemed disturbed at times, as if wondering what had happened to the boy he felt he knew.

"Wow, you've had a rough go of it, haven't you?" he said to me, "but I still don't understand why all this brings you to Turkey though?"

I finally had to tell him. "I'm here to visit the camps, Uncle."

Caught off guard as he was taking the final sip of his beer, he began to cough. "Are you okay?" I said.

"The camps? Why on earth would you do that? What good could possibly come from that?"

I had no choice but to tell him everything: the folders, the documents, the pictures, and notes. He looked at me differently as I laid out the facts and the path before me. I was no longer the innocent young boy he had known all his life and probably still thought of as. I was far from innocent. Innocence is like the silent peace that exists between two sides before the first shot is fired. After the silence has been pierced by the bullet, no matter what the outcome, silence will never feel the same again.

Things were out in the open by now and we were many drinks deep. If there is one good thing about alcohol, it is the honesty it induces. I told uncle about my life, about my distorted ego's pursuits. I confessed about the hold that women and sex had on me and the games I played with them. I told him how the unabashed pursuit of money forced me to sacrifice my integrity. I even told him about my experiences with drugs and the many long, dark nights spent under their devilish guise and influence. My uncle's look was rather somber. He looked at me differently, almost as if he didn't recognize me any longer.

"Uncle," I said to him, hoping for some response. He took a large sip of his beer and looked at me.

"You are your father's son, what did you expect?"

"What's that supposed to mean?" I yelled, catching myself and Uncle Ammad off guard. "I didn't mean to yell," I said apologetically. "I'm just tired of ruining my life and those of others due to my unresolved issues and past. I'm not happy about it all any longer."

"What aren't you happy about," he asked me.

"Everything!" I exclaimed. "Work, love, where I live. All of it."

I sat back against the booth; my body sank and my head dropped in defeat. He stared at me and I could see that my innocence was lost in his eyes.

"It's okay," he said, "It's going to be okay. Finish your beer and let's go," he said to me, motioning towards outside. He placed a few bills on the table and we made our way out into the night.

It was dark, and we were slightly inebriated. He pulled out a cigar and slowly lit it, gently turning it back and forth as the fire from the lighter scorched the tip, turning the tobacco amber orange. We walked in silence for five minutes sharing the stogie. I had wanted to break the silence, but the dynamics seemed to have completely changed now.

"I guess I don't know you as well as I thought I did," Uncle Ammad said, breaking the silence. "I love you still the same and I'm not here to judge, but to help."

I smiled at him, looking to my left where he was. We kept walking.

"I'm not perfect," he continued. "No one is. I've done things I'm not proud of either, nor am I living out my dream as I had envisaged as a child." He was staring at the ground as he spoke. Why do we stare down when we are unhappy or reflective? "When my father died several years ago, I went through a similar phase as you are now," he said to me. I resent it when others pretend to know how you're feeling or what you're going through.

He stopped, near a corner bustling with street salesman and hustlers. "Look," he said, facing me, "life gives us two options: get busy living, or get busy dying." I was moved by his words. There was an awkward silence. "You are like a son to me, so I will tell you what I can, but about the camps, I cannot help you with that." His expression turned solemn. "That's the past, young man, and the past is no longer."

"No, god damn it!" I yelled, surprising us both. "I'm sorry," I then said to him, feeling bad. "Look, Uncle Ammad, the past may be dead for you, but it's quite alive for me." Nodding in understanding, he motioned for us to continue walking. We started to pace again and turned onto another, busier street with cafes and shops and people around enjoying their night.

"The article you mentioned to me earlier," I had told him about the documents on the drive, "you know nothing about that?"

"Know nothing about what, Uncle?" I said in response.

He sighed. "I shouldn't be the one to tell you about this."

"Tell me about what?" I said to him, getting the impression that he was about to reveal something of significance to me. Eager to know, but nervous as well, I comported myself respectfully and stared at him.

"Let's go up this street," he gestured to his left up ahead.

I could not be prepared for what I was about to receive.

Uncle Ammad and his family had fled Iran about the same time as my family had in 1987. We met each other in the camps. He was there from the beginning and got to know my father quite well.

"Something big happened while we were all here, something that changed all our lives, something your father was responsible for."

I looked at him, head on. "Please, tell me everything."

Uncle filled me in about a major scandal between the Iranian and Turkish government in the late 1980s that we apparently had become embroiled in. "The Turkish government was being paid handsomely by our country to provide information about the many thousands of prominent Iranian intellectual refugees on its soil, such as your father, and to a lesser extent, me. The objective was to locate these individuals and repatriate them and their families back to Iran, where we would either be imprisoned or summarily executed."

I felt as though I was being told some fiction, but I wasn't.

Uncle continued. "The Turkish government shamefully participated by convincing refugees like us that they were boarding trains or buses headed to Europe or another safe haven, but which were in fact, headed back to Iranian soil."

It was too much to take in at once as conclusions began to dawn upon me. I asked my uncle to stop. "Give me a minute, please." Stepping aside, I took a few deep breaths.

"Are you alright?" my uncle asked me. I simply nodded. I was not an ignorant individual. I was quite aware of the evils of the world of men.

"Uncle," I said, looking at him, disconcerted, flummoxed, "what the hell does all this have to do with my father?" Our eyes were locked, and they spoke much, silently.

Sighing, he took a deep breath. "Let's keep walking," he said to me. A homeless, disheveled man appeared before us a few steps ahead sitting down on the curb. Reaching out with his hand and dirtied cup, he asked us for change. My uncle stopped and dropped him some. "That could easily have been us," he said to me with a heavy look. Indeed, it could have. Life is random like that. Who knew what landed that man on the street? Who knows what's landed us where we are?

Nearing the waterfront, we had become estranged and silent towards one another. Perhaps it was the alcohol. Perhaps it's the discomfort we feel around the truth sometimes. I could not stay silent any longer. "Well, uncle," I said to him, stopping to get his attention. He pointed forward towards the walkway by the water. "We'll have more privacy there, less distractions."

The wind had picked up as it funneled faster and closer to the water. It was a rather still night, which I welcomed. I could see the lights of the east side of Istanbul across from us. Reflecting on the water, they grew elongated and warped, creating a collage of colours, each blending into the other like the millions of lives in this great and ancient city. Who doesn't love the sparkle of civilization?

Uncle Ammad broke the silence at last. "Your father, may he rest in peace, being the talented journalist and investigator that he was, began to realize what was happening while in the camps. He started to add the pieces together. When he did, he knew that he would either be assassinated or led back to Iran and to the demise of your family and your lives.

I listened intently. "He came to a group of us and revealed his findings in trust. He presented us with his plans. He wanted as many of us as possible to follow him to the United Nations consulate in Istanbul with our families, where he would have local reporters and photographers present. He would shine light on our cause and that of our peoples and the ignominious arrangement between Turkey and Iran. He even vowed to kill himself with a razor if that's what it took. Your father never bluffed."

There was a pause. Unsure of how to digest it all, I reached for my cigarettes, but fumbled and dropped them. I dropped my head next, covering my face in frustration. "Why did mother not tell me this all these years?" I said. "How could they keep this from me?"

"You know your family loves you and only means to protect you."

"Bullshit," I said, upset, "that's bullshit. They had no right to keep this from me." My family knew I had always wanted to know more about my past, and it angered me that they did not respect this enough to tell me the truth all these years. Turning around to face him, I asked him where he was in this all. His look seemed long, deep like the sea from where the river before us drew its water.

"I couldn't do it," he said to me, unable to look me in the eyes. "None of us could. Your father was incredibly courageous and fearless. We were all too afraid to make such a bold stand."

I was puzzled. "So what happened then?"

"Well," he replied, "he did it himself. He did it alone, with you guys of course."

I was dumbfounded. This contradicted the image I had always held of my father as a selfish, sordid, and deranged man. This was far too humanitarian and selfless. It didn't make sense to me.

"What was the outcome of it all?" I asked my uncle.

What I heard next would forever change all my notions about my father, myself, my life.

"Well," he began to say as he paced past me, stammering his words, unable to speak clearly, "he saved us. He saved many of us." My uncle looked at me with tears in his eyes. "After the incident, he made national newspapers and magazines." I presumed he was referring to the ones that I had in my possession in the folders I had received back in Toronto. "Your father utilized all of his connections and resources in journalism and politics to pull off a coup for Iranian refugees and create a nightmare for the Turkish government. Whole diplomatic channels were opened up as a result of his actions, his bravery. He was immediately offered amnesty and protection from various entities and governments. It was a truly remarkable feat. Your father was a true hero. He really was."

My heart felt heavy, like a brick in my chest, weighing me down. Tears streamed from my eyes. I lost my balance and felt the ground shake beneath me. Scouring, I noticed a bench nearby. I walked towards it and sat down. My uncle followed suit, placing his arms around me.

"I'm sorry I had to be the one to tell you this. I truly am," he said.

I felt completely overwhelmed by the weight of this revelation. My uncle had just completely upended the image I had of my father and painted him out to be a person that I never knew he was. I never met this man. There was good in him; he couldn't have been my father, could he? I felt quite guilty, realizing that I had mistreated my father while he was alive on false grounds, but how could I know he had done such things?

"Uncle," I said, "please tell me more."

"You've had enough for a day, young man. We can continue tomorrow."

"No," I said curtly, catching my breath. "Tell me now, please."

He stared at me for a moment and began to speak again. "Your father, emboldened by his success, requested that all the families within the immediate section of the camp we were staying in be given the same protection and asylum. The scandal had made news outside of Turkey and brought your father significant leverage. Many families, countless women and children, including, of course, me and your aunt, were given several options of amnesty, including Canada."

I started to piece the conclusion together myself by this point. "Your father saved a lot of people, and for that, I will forever be indebted and grateful to him, as will many others."

I could have been a weeping statue at that moment. I could barely move from the shock of what I had just been told. I could faintly hear my uncle say something in Farsi. It must have been a prayer for my father. I made a valiant attempt to fight my emotions, but could not. I succumbed to the many blows. Crying now, my body was in convulsions, and I could barely breathe. Uncle Ammad grabbed me from the opposing shoulder, twisting me around and bringing me into him with a force that betrayed his small frame. I did not resist, I could not. I lacked the strength to do so. The confluence of recent events, mixed with the past events that I had just become aware of, was simply too much to bear all at once. It is in moments like this that we turn to our partners, our lovers, our soulmates. Anastasya was no longer here for me, however, which accentuated the pain and loneliness I felt just now, despite my uncle's presence. Who was my father after all? What more lay buried with him? Could it be that there was indeed good or love in him?

Slowly, I began to catch my breath and control my thoughts. My uncle, holding me close all along, slowly released me from his grip. We looked at one another for a moment then and there, our eyes speaking volumes, our lips sealed like the ocean floor.

"Let's go home," he said to me. I said nothing, but nodded my head. "Everything is going to be fine, I promise." I looked at him, a blank stare on my face devoid of emotion.

"Don't make promises about things you can't control."

He smiled, laughing ever so faintly, slapping my face gently with his left hand. "Stubborn, just like your old man," he said smiling. "Things have a funny way of working out in the end," he said to me. Everyone says that, naively, I thought. What if they don't?

"If in the morning, you still want to visit the camps, I will take you," he said. I nodded. Uncle Ammad now stood up, motioned for me to do the same, helping me. Inhaling deeply, I adjusted my jacket, composing myself as best as I could. I felt the wind caress my face just then. In fact I heard it. They say that spirits travel with the wind. We began walking back towards the car.

Chapter 5:
Affinity

Waking up, I didn't feel so great, but I noticed my father's files and documents strewn about me around the couch. I saw a picture of my father in another Turkish newspaper and realized quickly why I felt the way I did. It was the sheer weight of what I had discovered about his life the previous night, and by extension, mine. As quickly as I recalled it all, I became angry at my mother and older sisters for keeping me in the dark about the truth.

Making my way upstairs, it was still early morning, just coming up on 9 a.m. Daylight had flooded the home once more through the many windows in the house. Walking towards the kitchen, leaving foot stains on the impeccably clean, dark brown, oak floors, I heard the ruffle of newspaper, and to my surprise, encountered Uncle Ammad sitting at the table reading.

"Good morning," he said to me.

"Morning, uncle. Aren't you supposed to be at work?" I responded.

Completely deferring my question, he revealed his face, putting down the newspaper.

"How did you sleep, Moshe?"

I shrugged in response; I hadn't slept much or well.

"So you didn't sleep?" he said to me, as I walked towards the coffee machine that had half a flask of freshly brewed java, whose rich aroma permeated the room.

"No, I slept just fine," I lied.

"How about some breakfast?" he asked me. "I'm not your aunt, but I'm pretty talented with a skillet and some eggs!" He was pointing to the stove. I walked over and had a look, but wasn't enticed by what I saw. Appetite emanates first from the mind, not the stomach.

"Perhaps later, uncle."

By now I had figured out what it was he was trying to do: help me get my day started on the right note and lift the weight of the previous night from me somewhat. I knew what I had committed to doing today, but I was having second thoughts, nervous just thinking about that place. My mug was shaking; my hands were not quite still. Uncle noticed this, leading to an awkward exchange between us. The camps were forever seared into my mind because of what had happened there to me, which only my mother to this day knew about.

"Don't make me take you there, please, just leave it in the past."

I nodded and told him I had to confront my past and my demons once and for all. Uncle leaned in and said, "What your father did to you was not your fault!"

Of course, he didn't know what I was referring to, what happened on that one occasion to me at the camps, and other things growing up. No one can truly know another person's life. Everyone says that about the past it seems. To leave it behind. Deep down, I agreed with him, I always had. The past is like the cocoon from which a moth is born, the moth the present. Once it has emerged, the moth no longer needs the past in which it once lived, as it no longer serves any purpose; it no longer exists.

It is so much harder than it sounds, however, and every single person knows this. Society today foists this concept upon us in varied ways. Where did you go to school, where have you worked, where have you been, what have you achieved, and so on and so forth. It is almost as if we collectively make ourselves beholden to the past and not engaged with the present or the future. At least it feels this way to me.

Coming up on noon, we had been stuck in traffic on the western outskirts of Istanbul, where the camps were located. Becoming rather anxious as we neared the general area, a rather bleak and dreary, almost industrial place, I took a clonazepam. My uncle noticed, shooting a worried glance over at me, catching me staring back at him with the corner of my eye.

"They help me calm down," I said. He continued to stare at me. Eyes back on the road, a main building appeared in sight, which I faintly remembered, or at least thought I did. It was obvious that much work had been done on these facilities, not a surprise given the time that had elapsed since I was last here. Recalling the large, bulky, design-less exterior of the main building, which housed the administrative offices of this compound, I knew without even looking that to my right were large, perhaps three-story walls that housed the many separate buildings which comprised the camps and contained the living units for families and refugees.

"Can you believe we used to live here, uncle," I said to him with a look of astonishment on my face. My uncle pulled up as far as he could and stopped near the gate entrance to drop me off.

"Okay, here you are." I gulped. "You sure you want to do this? It's not too late to turn around, you know." I looked at him, looked at the austere metallic gate, then at my hands, beginning to shake ever so slightly again as they always did when I got nervous. I closed my eyes for a moment, trying to gather strength.

"No, uncle," I said, "I have to do this. I'll be fine. Thanks."

He was disappointed, but didn't fight me. "Alright then, you call me if you need anything, anything at all, you hear me?"

I nodded in agreement. "Thank you, uncle," I said affectionately, for a moment looking upon him as a father figure. Uncle Ammad was truly a good man. There was no lying to him. Intelligent, but not deep, he appreciated life, but wasn't consumed by it. Not like father or me. I envied this about him. We all envy the calm in others, I thought, looking at him as he stared directly at the camp gate, probably recalling his time here also.

"You're going to get out or should I shove you?" he said, smiling at me; I smiled back at him. I attempted to get out of the car, but was painfully held in place by my seatbelt, which I completely forgot to unlatch. We both looked at each other and started laughing. There is truly no other act that is more life affirming than laughter, something we don't do enough of; any of us.

"Okay, let's try this again," I said as I unlatched the belt and stepped out, looking at my uncle and smiling before closing the door. I walked up to the gate, spoke with the attendant, showed my ID, and proceeded onto the grounds through a smaller door to the left of the gate. Looking back, uncle was still there. I moved forward about 50 feet to the main building and walked up the stairs, turning around to see my uncle finally drive away. I felt alone again.

Inside the building, taking a deep breath, I looked for an information desk or kiosk. None were around, so I asked one of the janitors near me, an older man with greasy, curly long hair who had been mopping the floor. He guided me downstairs without saying anything to a corridor that led to an office where some officials were present. I followed his directions and appeared before a large office with an attendant behind a desk, a young lady with dark brown hair and a blue suit, presumably a uniform.

Approaching her, I grunted to get her attention. She looked up at me with a rather cold, emotionless face.

"May I help you?" she said to me in an unusually thick voice for a female.

"Yes, hi," I responded, "I was hoping to speak with someone regarding some individuals who had long ago stayed here for a period of time."

She sat still, staring at me blankly. "I'm sorry, sir, but who are you?"

Not sure I knew how to answer, I simply replied with my name. "Moshe Asham." I felt quite stupid for doing so afterwards, rolling my eyes quickly to my left, but then back at her.

She remained quiet for a bit as if to acknowledge my stupidity, then clarified: "No, as in your title, what political organization do you work for, which entity are you representing?"

I hadn't much thought about it until now, but it wasn't an unreasonable question, considering the nature of this place. "Actually, I'm not affiliated with any," I said. "I used to be a refugee here many, many years ago myself. I was hoping that I could get some information about me and my family. Please."

For a second, I thought to myself, "What are you doing, Moshe? You can't just walk in here and ask for such information, you idiot." I had no choice but to, so I maintained my appearance, literally. I wondered what she was thinking of me at that moment.

"Wait here one moment, sir," she said as she got up and walked away. I began walking around the room, looking at various posters and reviewing various brochures and pamphlets. No one else was present. I could ascertain from various logos around the room that this was still partially a UN initiative, as UNHCR was evident on many of the collateral, as was the trademark of the Government of Turkey, along with several other NGOs, many of which I did not recognize.

After 5-10 minutes, a loud voice startled me and I turned around. "Hello, sir." I was looking at a large, bulky, perhaps 40-year-old man standing beside the female attendant I had originally been speaking with. He was also an official of some sort, which I gathered from his attire and hat.

"Hello," I responded.

"You are looking for information about your family, I understand?" he said to me, stepping forward a few feet. "You have stayed here in the past, I am told?"

I stepped forward. "Yes," I responded, clearing my voice with a cough, "many years ago, between 1988-1989."

Nodding his head, he said, "Ah, okay. Iranian?"

"Yes," I responded quickly, but I answered back with hesitation. "Well, I am a Canadian citizen, but I am of Iranian descent." We had a standoff for a moment. He was rather intimidating, I had to admit.

Finally, he broke the silence. "Come with me, please."

I spent about 30 minutes with this man in his office. He was friendlier and more helpful than he had seemed at first. I had opened up to him about who I was, where I was from, my family's story, really my father's story. He was quite intrigued by it all; who wouldn't be. I gathered that he was in his 40s, but I certainly wasn't going to ask him. He was built large, a thick upper body with broad shoulders and tanned skin, short black hair, and thick sharp eyebrows, every part chiseled like a soldier. I was told that what I was doing was rather unconventional, that normally those who came looking for information were with an organization and had some form of clearance or certification. Clearly I did not, so I shared some of my father's documents which I had brought along, hoping it might persuade him to assist me. I even showed him the magazine which contained an old picture of this very facility and relayed the role my father played in revealing the large and scandalous covert operation between the Iranian and Turkish regimes, which saved my family and many others. I could sense that he was a man of morals and ethics, as he had religious scriptures on the walls and a holy book on his table, along with a certain tough, but congenial demeanour. He was, however, ostensibly kind and compassionate. He advised me that normally they would not be forthcoming with their files, but given my story, the documents I had with me, and clear proof that I was in fact who I claimed to be, he saw no reason in not assisting me, especially given that I had come so far to obtain whatever information I could.

Breathing a sigh of relief at all this, I realized that the universe had been kind to me. Sadly, he was unable to draw up anything of real value for me, other than an electronic copy of my family's file merely confirming that we were indeed residents at this camp during those years, the names of my sisters and mother, and our critical information and such, but nothing more. He did tell me that the officer who managed our file at the time and would have had some direct contact with my father was still active at the camp and may be able to assist me further. My eyes lit up at this prospect of hope.

"Could I speak with this man?" I asked promptly, excited, eyes thick with interest. He simply stared at me, as if I had asked something inappropriate, and perhaps I may have. "It would mean a lot to me, sir."

There was another pause, but shorter this time as he spoke.

"It could be arranged, but it may be tricky. His office is located deeper inside the compound where only employees, officials, or volunteers can enter."

We both sat there in silence for a moment. He reclined in his chair, playing with his pen and looking at the ceiling, throwing me off guard as he seemed almost childish, much different than the stiff official of a minute ago.

An idea came to me just then, forcing me forward in my seat. "I will volunteer!" I said excitedly, as if I had made a discovery of importance. I startled him as his head fell back on me rather quickly, bringing down and forth his wider body. He dropped his pen as well. I felt nervous all of a sudden, tightening up.

"I'm sorry" I said immediately. "I didn't mean to startle you."

He picked his pen up from the floor and stared at me. I became tense and uneasy, however, about this idea. How could I volunteer at this place? All of a sudden, like a rush of blood to the head, I realized that I was so caught up searching for answers that I forgot where I was. I loathed this place. It terrified me. This person in front of me, he could just as easily be the same type of person as the one many years ago who stole my innocence from me here in one heinous act. I lost my composure and it was obvious. The official was looking at me suspiciously. He hadn't said anything yet, but I could tell he was probing me visually, trying to figure me out, yet he said absolutely nothing, unless you counted eye contact as conversation. He said quite a bit with that language.

I had to be quick, I had to react, and I could not retract what I had just said, so I doubled up, "Yes, I would like to become a volunteer," I said again. "Can you arrange this for me?"

His expression changed ever so slightly into a more amiable one. "Well," he said, "normally there would be a lengthy process for this, but I will come up with a way to get around it for you."

Surprised, I smiled at him. "Thank you so much, sir," I said to him as I leaned forward. "I can't tell you what this means to me."

He stared back at me, not obliging my gratitude. "I'm not sure why I am helping you, young man, but something tells me I should. Clearly, your father was a great man, and in his honour, I will grant you this favour."

Finding it hard to stomach the word's "father" and "great man" together in the same line, I simply nodded without showing emotion. I thought about why he might say such a thing, but then realized quickly that he had seen the article in the magazine and could obviously read it, as it was in Turkish. It made sense. Thinking about it, I presumed there must also be something about all this on the file he had just called up on his computer. I wondered what more might be in there that I did not yet know. The irony of it all was not lost on me. My father was in some way helping me with my investigation about him. The thought alone gave me shudders.

"Thank you, sir," I said to him again, unsure of what else to say.

"You can thank God," he said to me, "not me."

I simply nodded again. I wasn't sure about God anymore. Like the rest of my generation, I was also disillusioned with religion. I wondered often how anyone practiced any religion anymore, or whether they still believed in a deity. We all pay lip service to it, but how often do we actually think about these things anymore? Do we still believe in God? Have we use for providence anymore in our modern world? My philosophical musings were quickly interrupted as he picked up the phone and placed a call then. He chatted with someone for a few minutes. I became nervous. What were they talking about? What if he was calling the police? That was ridiculous; I had done nothing wrong. I sat there silently, trying to remain calm, my hands on my lap, looking around the room in vain. His pace, his general way of being, body posture, tone of voice, mannerism and expressions, those small details that distinguish one soul from another, it was all rather calm and proportioned for a man of his size and stature.

He finally placed the phone down and motioned for me to head out with him. "We're going upstairs." He said it so quickly and sharply, moving in the same fashion that I felt as though he was a drill sergeant. Gathering my documents quickly, I followed him out, past the young lady who was still at the front desk and down the corridor back upstairs.

We entered an austere office area with a few workers inside at various desks. The area was a cluttered environment containing very old PCs and a musty smell reminiscent of barbershops. The officer whose name I realized I did not know walked in with force and stood at the front of the room, yelling something out, ostensibly a name.

"Kanda."

Right away, a young, attractive female responded, getting up from her desk at the back of the room and walking over towards us in a graceful manner.

"Moshe, meet Kanda. She works with the refugees and guests directly."

I was transfixed by this young female before me, even startled, as if I had met her before, which was not possible. I could not come up with one word to utter; I was completely tongue-twisted. Was I attracted to her or was it something else? She was certainly rather attractive, even endearing, a smile as resplendent as a Mediterranean sunset. Had we met before? No, no, that could not be possible, our lives divided by oceans. This moment became awkward as I continued to stare at her, unable to relent, and her at me, though less amorously and more amiably.

The officer was looking at me with a look of displeasure, mixed with confusion, raising his left brow and crossing his arms, perhaps starting to regret being so forthcoming with me. I blinked, a bit worried, throwing him a light smile to ease the tension, scared to look at her, and him.

She finally interjected, breaking the tension and my gaze. "A pleasure to meet you, Moshe." She extended her hand out to me. Forcing myself to come to quickly, I extended my hand out also, reaching hers. Her hands were soft like rose petals. I looked over at the officer coyly and quickly then back at her.

"A pleasure indeed, Tanda," I said to her. "Pardon me, its Kanda, not Tanda." Embarrassed, I was flush red, looking at her directly. "Oh, yes, of course, forgive me, Kanda."

Anything positive I had established with the officer must have been lost on me, I thought. In fact, he had not once taken his eyes off me since he introduced me to this beautiful young girl. Looking at him nervously, I noticed his brows were furrowed and he was suspicious.

Wanting to explain, but unable to, I simply said, "Pardon me, I haven't slept much in the past few days" to both of them. His staring continued unabated. It left me feeling rather uncomfortable, like a kid in school getting scolded in front of his whole class. We've all certainly been there. These are formative experiences of life. No one said anything for a moment, and the awkwardness returned.

"I understand you'll be volunteering with us," she finally said, removing some tension.

"Yes," I responded quickly, with a smile, staring at him first, then back at her. "I'm looking forward to it."

"Great, we can always use another set of hands around here. Just some paperwork to complete for now and then we can get you set up for access to the grounds and an orientation."

Smiling at her, I nodded. The officer's eyes were still fixed on me, albeit a bit less skeptically, but he finally spoke, breaking the silence.

"You are in good hands with Kanda. I will see you tomorrow perhaps. Make good use of your time here and use it for what you need to do, not what you might want to."

His eyes rolled again as he said this, and I understood the insinuation. Was it that obvious I was attracted to this young woman? Probably, but it did not matter. I was here on important and meaningful business.

"Yes, sir, tomorrow. Absolutely," I responded, smiling at him. Another pause, he looked at me head on and at first confused, I quickly made sense of it and got out of his way.

"Good evening to you both."

I watched him walk away and out of the office. He was certainly a character, one I owed a debt of gratitude to already. Turning back, I saw her again, Kanda.

"Follow me," she said with a most effervescent smile. She sat at her desk, gesturing to the chair opposite her, welcoming me. "Please, take a seat." I smiled and did as asked. "Don't worry about him. He's much warmer than his demeanour might suggest," she said.

"Yes, he's a nice guy," I retorted, continuing to stare at this young lady who had so captivated me, as if she was some apparition, some mirage in the desert in which I was lost.

She had light brunette hair that was long and wavy at the tips, like incoming waves on a beach. Her face was round, but very well proportioned, with rosy cheeks and the most unforgettable dimples. Her smile was chiseled by the masters themselves. Her eyes, large and hazel, were like those of a reindeers. One could easily get lost in them. Her skin was fair and seemed smoother than fine porcelain; her teeth were perfectly aligned and marble white. She beamed with the essence of a mermaid from the sea. Her frame was short, but well-rounded. Her hands were tiny as they punched into the keyboard ever so lightly with a certain delicateness as if she was knitting a child's coat. One could hardly hear the noise of the keyboard when she did, that's how subtle she was. She seemed too perfect, and in life, often when something seems that way, it usually is. I felt as though I was possessed by her, and I may well have been. For 10-15 minutes, I did this, adoring her in my mind, while cooperating with her as she asked me some basic questions and details.

"All done" she said now as she punched the enter button on the keyboard. "We'll just run some basic background checks using your passport, which should be approved overnight, hopefully providing us with clearance by the morning."

She was so ebullient and seemingly happy, which confounded me, considering where she worked.

"Great," I managed to respond back, which was indeed delightful news to me, as I had anticipated more trouble gaining access to this place. It wasn't your local library after all.

"I understand you stayed her many years ago?" she asked me.

My expression changed quickly. "Yes, many years ago, 23 to be exact."

She looked at me, a bit deeper than before. She was thinking something; I could tell by the fact that she was fidgeting with her hands, a telltale sign of mental activity.

"Your father," she said, "he seemed like a great man, a real hero."

I was hearing this again. My father, the monster who tortured me and my family all of our lives, being referred to as a great man, a hero twice in one day. It was unsettling.

I quickly changed the conversation. "It's been a long day for me. Can we pick up again tomorrow?" I had achieved what I needed to here today; in fact, I had done quite well.

Somewhat caught off guard, she seemed smart enough to infer that I obviously did not want to discuss my father or my past anymore. "I understand" she said with a half-smile. A moment of silence ensued. "Well," she said, "I've got your number. We'll call you later tonight."

I smiled and nodded, continuing to stare at her long after.

"Will I be seeing you tomorrow, Kanda?"

"Yes," she responded, "perhaps, but if I am not around, there are others who can provide you with assistance."

"Yes, I'm sure, but I would prefer it if you could assist me, please."

She looked at me, inquisitively, a straight face revealing to me that smiling was not her sole expression.

"If I am available, I would be happy to do so."

I smiled at these words. "Great. Thank you. I will see you first thing in the morning then. Good night."

"Not unless we call you, remember" she said now, stopping me in my tracks as I was about to get up.

"Yes, of course." Maybe she wasn't a mermaid after all, I thought to myself.

"Good evening." she said to me. Turning around. I walked towards the door, stopping just before I reached it. I turned around to see if she was staring at me at all. To my disappointment, she was not. I had a moment of resoluteness, however, and needed to ask her a question. I was perplexed by this woman. I clearly had an affinity to her. I walked back to where she sat, standing above her. She hadn't noticed me approaching.

"I'm sorry, but may I ask you a question, Kanda?" She jumped slightly; I had caught her off guard. "Forgive me," I said right away.

"Okay, sure," she responded. "Ask."

"How do you continue to smile working in such a place, day in and day out?"

There was a pause.

"You want to know the truth?"

I nodded.

Every, single day above ground, is a good one.

"I can't believe you just said that."

"Why not? You asked me."

That might have been the most remarkable response to a question I had ever heard in my life. I stood there, unable to say anything more.

"Look," she said to me, "there's a lot of dirt and filth in the world as far as it concerns us humans. We can either roll around in it like pigs, or we can clean it up."

I wasn't sure if I was turned on or off by this language from this woman who had so smitten me. A bit of both I reckoned. I had received much more than I had bargained for or anticipated coming here today. I couldn't deny it. I felt something for this beautiful young woman. Something I hadn't felt in some time. I could barely recall Anastasya just now. Love is fickle, I thought to myself. Perhaps it was never love with her, perhaps it was just lust. Lust is certainly fickle too. How often nowadays do we misinterpret one for the other in our sexually depraved society? Considering the rate of success for marriages, I sometimes wondered if love and marriage weren't endangered species. It didn't matter. I felt something very meaningful right now about her, this young woman, Kanda. I could not deny her pull on me. I felt butterflies in my stomach. Don't butterflies carry love?

Chapter 6:
Paradise Lost

It was another sun kissed morning in Istanbul. I smiled as we drove once more towards the camps. Yesterday's experience there had given me a boost, and I was in good spirits. After another fine meal prepared by my aunt the previous night, along with several bottles of wine, me and my family talked and shared many laughs. I felt as though perhaps there was hope for life and for me after all. Smiling as I thought back on the night, it dawned upon me just now that the small and simple things are all that really matter; there's really nothing bigger.

That wasn't all of it, however. There was something else front and centre on my mind - Kanda. My encounter with this young woman had left a profound impact on me, which I could not deny.

"Same area?" my uncle said to me as we drove up the road towards the main building, interrupting my thoughts.

"Oh, yes," I said to him, "same area as yesterday, please."

"So as a volunteer," he said, "what exactly are you required to do? What are your tasks?"

I was caught off guard and unsure how to respond. After all, I had only volunteered so that I could gain access to the camps.

"I presume typical activities," I said looking at him, then back at the road. "You know, maybe preparing accommodations, food, paper work, etc."

He didn't look convinced, taking his eyes off the road and placing them directly on mine. Sometimes we get caught lying, but we know it and so does the other party, yet we go on lying anyways. It happens more often than we care to admit.

Now I began to have second thoughts myself about all this. What the hell was I doing here anyways? Was it a good idea? I felt drawn to this place, however, because of my past and especially because of this young woman whom I had yesterday met, Kanda. I was eager to see her again. I felt as we all do when we have our first crush and look forward to school the next day, because we know we will see them, despite the fact that we hate school itself.

He pulled up to the same spot as he had yesterday and I got out of the car. "Good luck," my uncle said to me, enthusiastically with two thumbs up, being facetious.

"Thanks for the lift, uncle," I said in response. I turned around and walked past the gate, up the stairs, and back into the building.

Everything was the same as the day before, right down to the janitor. I walked downstairs first to the main administrative office where I had gone yesterday. Walking in, I saw the officer standing near the window, speaking to a few others. He noticed me and simply pointed for me to step back into the hallway and motioned with one finger that he required a moment. I did as he asked, waiting outside the room.

"Good morning," he said to me, drawing my attention quickly as he came out towards me.

"Good morning," I responded. A slight pause ensued as we stared at each other.

"You made it," he finally said. "That's good."

I nodded in reply.

"Upstairs, same office as yesterday. They are expecting you."

Continuing to look at him, I eventually acknowledged and thanked him, making my way upstairs.

Now walking down a separate hallway towards the office where I had met Kanda yesterday, anxious and eager to see her again, I felt a skip in my heart. As I arrived at the room and approached the door slowly, I was saddened as she was nowhere in sight.

"Can I help you, sir?" one of the other young ladies said to me, whom I gazed upon with a look of confusion on my face.

"Yes, hi, I'm, I'm looking for..." and before I could finish, someone tapped me from behind, turning me around, much to my delight to countenance once more this beautiful and endearing young lady. My smile must have been broad as a watermelon slice. I inhaled deeply before I said anything.

"Good morning."

Smiling back, she said in response, "Good morning." I stood still, simply gazing upon her as if some mural at the Louvre. "So obviously your paperwork checked out. I will just need you to sign a few documents before we can proceed," she said as she led the way to her desk. She didn't seem as warm as she was yesterday. Maybe it was just me. I signed several documents, which I scarcely even looked over. Do we ever look over things we sign, after all?

"Thank you," she said. "That should do it. Here is your badge for the day until we get you a permanent one." She reached over, grabbing my blue buttoned shirt by the opening of the neck ever so gently with her supple hands to pin the badge to my left chest area, then patted it for good measure. I simply continued staring at her.

"Thank you," I said to her, not even bothering to look at the badge and keeping my eyes fixed on hers.

She smiled. "You're welcome," she said. "Well, I've actually got a lighter schedule than normal today, I'll be able to give you a tour myself if you are alright with that?"

I laughed inside. Did she know how drawn I was to her? Did she feel anything towards me?

"Yes, of course. I would like that very much." I said to her, smiling. She led the way and I followed.

Now stepping into a new area of the camp I had not yet been to, but remaining inside the same compound, Kanda gave me a brief history and explained to me where we would be heading today.

"This particular area of the camp is for families who have been displaced by war from countries ranging from Afghanistan to the Congo, really quite a wide range, but all active war zones." She was clearly intelligent, she knew quite a bit about conflict zones and the political/economic origins of them, a part of her job I supposed.

"Have you visited any of these countries?" I asked her.

"Yes, I have."

"Were you ever afraid of being in harm's way?"

"No, I was not," she said, turning to motion for us to continue walking. She didn't seem keen on speaking in depth, that was for sure. I wondered why. We approached a gated area where a startling sight greeted us: two armed guards holding large, black semi-automatic machine guns.

"Wait here, please," she said. I did as I was instructed while she approached one and began speaking in Turkish and providing him with some documents. The guard looked up at me, rather ominously, forcing me to gulp and look away. After a moment, she motioned for me to come forward, which I quickly did, catching a brief glance of this tall, stocky character before walking through the gates.

"They are just precautionary," she said, catching me look back as we walked away, my tension palpable. I felt embarrassed for a moment in her presence. We turned a sharp right and walked down a long flight of stairs towards the end of which I noticed daylight. Before long, we were outside in a wide open area, slightly grassy, slightly muddy, the ground not uniform with three small roads leading to various large sections of this camp and its facilities, much of which I did not recall so well. Realizing exactly where I was, a heavy feeling overcame me and I stood still, taking a few deep breaths and surveying this place with wide open eyes.

She walked over to me, placing her hand on my left arm. "If at any point you want to turn back, please don't hesitate to tell me, okay?" she said affectionately.

I looked at her and smiled. "No, no, I'm fine, Kanda, just trying to absorb things, that's all. It's been 23 years."

A faint smile on her warm and welcoming visage, she nodded in agreement. Just then, a small grey vehicle, very much like a golf cart, arrived. We got on board and drove five minutes towards the centre building where apparently the guard I needed to speak with was located. Surveying my surroundings, I wondered why these types of facilities always looked so austere and dull. Why couldn't the builders paint them in yellow and green and blue, perhaps, I thought in earnest? Why were they always big block structures, straight lines and contours, dimly lit with poor exteriors that lack any essence and in the most depressing of colours? It's almost as if the buildings are built to sympathize with the plight of their tenants.

Taking my attention off them for a moment, I looked at this beautiful, remarkable young woman in front of me, riding with the driver. Her rich, brunette hair was dancing in the draft created by our forward motion, painting her like a princess riding a chariot. She was conversing with the driver in an animated manner, creating all forms of facial expressions, all ingratiating to me. Her body language, her strong use of her arms, all this suggested to me a woman full of passion and vigour. Though she was quiet – the most remarkable ones are – she had a zest and zeal all her own. I was quite taken by her, I had to admit to myself at that moment. There was just something about Kanda. How could she smile and remain so calm and giving when this is what she had to live through and be immersed in everyday? Was it just a façade? Was she hiding some deep pain and trauma herself that she was dealing with in this manner, by being here? If there was one thing I had come to learn about people in general thus far in life, it was that appearances are indeed often deceiving. Life is a real play after all, like theatre, and we are all playing two roles: who we really are in private, and who we portray ourselves to be in public.

We reached our building and disembarked our vehicle. It was a taller structure than it appeared from afar. Foreboding, in fact, as I veered up while walking in, almost as if I was entering some prison, or some medieval castle. We walked in past another guard, unarmed this time. Nearing a large double door, I could hear quite a bit of noise and commotion. She punched in a code on the terminal on the wall and pushed the doors open, revealing a long interior that was full of people. I walked in slowly and absorbed what was before me. We were on the second floor; it seemed as there was a balcony and two other floors above me. To the sides, there were little rooms that were clearly makeshift residences for whole families. They varied in size, but many of them couldn't have been larger than a one-bedroom apartment. It became clear to me quickly that this was a communal facility. There was a certain dankness in the air, a lack of breathable air almost. How did anyone sleep here, I thought to myself?

"Let's continue," Kanda said, curtly snapping me out of the hypnosis this place was putting me under. "This way," she motioned with an amiable look. I followed her like a lemming, walking along the balcony towards the centre where I could see an administrative area and where I was hoping I might find the guard whom I was in search of and perhaps cut short my visit here. It was more difficult than I imagined. We men like to play bold and fearless, but we're not nearly as strong as women and we know this, but we all play along anyways. I was sure by now Kanda had been advised that I was, in fact, volunteering for a particular purpose, but it hadn't seemed to bother her; she didn't seem to judge me for it at least.

We stopped as we approached a young boy who was standing near the railing, playing with a toy car. Kanda bent down to him, warmly greeting the little boy, who must have been no older than 5 or 6.

"Hello, Shuaib. How are you today, little man?" she said ever so affectionately, her tone changing from semi-reserved to unabashed mother figure just like that. She was like a chameleon and I loved each side of her. The boy gave her a hug and then displayed his toy to her with pride, as most children are keen on doing. Don't we all want to show off our belongings after all?

She spent a moment with this young boy, speaking with him, though he seemed to say nothing back. Was he mute, I thought to myself? I felt only sympathy for the boy, knowing that his life was not going to be easy. Our species has a way of pitying those less fortunate quietly, all the while subconsciously feeling better about ourselves for it. For the first time in at least a day, I felt my anxiety start to rear its ugly head. This boy could well have been me many years ago. Was I looking at myself? She looked at me and gestured for me to come over and say hello. Of course I obliged, walking towards him with a smile. To my dismay, however, the boy reacted by running away into the room in front of him as I neared. Confused, I was unsure what this meant.

"Don't worry about him. He's not used to meeting anyone new," she reassured me.

"Understandable," I nodded, looking down.

"Excuse me," she said to me as she walked forward and into the same room. Unsure what to do, I too stepped forward to have a look inside gently, witnessing a sight that sank my heart and mood. A woman, 45 years old or so I gathered, was sitting on a decrepit bed with an infant in her arms, while two young children slept on the other bed and, of course, Shuaib, who was sitting on the ground near some plastic toys, playing quietly. It was the picture of sadness and hardship, this woman's life. Though I knew nothing about it, I could sense it acutely. The utter plight she must have endured thus far and did so still daily. For a moment, I saw my mother in her, knowing full well she had been in a similar position many years ago. I saw myself in Shuaib.

My anxiety overwhelmed me as I felt nauseous and developed the spins, quickly retreating a few steps back and out of the room, placing my back against the immediate wall outside for support. Reaching into my pocket, I grabbed a clonazepam, which I had strategically placed there, anticipating that I would need it today, and popped it quickly, closing my eyes as if to escape to another place, trying to catch my breath. Not wanting Kanda to see me like this, I tried my best to regain my footing. My eyes remained shut, as this whole place was becoming all too recognizable and painful for me. "Breathe," I whispered to myself repeatedly. "Breathe."

A moment later, Kanda had come out and seen me and became quite alarmed at the sight before her.

"Are you alright? Can I do something to help?"

Forcing myself upright, I fought to compose myself as best as I could and reassured her that I was fine.

"I'll be alright, its passing." I took a few minutes and worked myself back to normalcy. She suggested we proceed to the office to find the officer I was here to see so that I could leave as soon as possible. That was thoughtful of her.

"Listen," she said to me, "don't feel upset with yourself or embarrassed." Was it that obvious, I thought? "It's normal" she continued, "given your history here, it's completely understandable."

I only smiled back at her. She warmed my soul with her every word. Each sentence was like a blanket, covering me in her radiant heat. She had a word with the mother she was tending to who clearly seemed puzzled by this all, leaving me feeling even worse.

"Let's go" she motioned, tilting her neck in the direction of the office ever so slightly.

"Are you sure?" I said as I pointed to the lady.

She smiled and said, "Yes. I'll come back to them. I'm not going anywhere."

We proceeded to the office, walking about 50 yards perhaps before finally arriving. It was much like the office in the main building where I had met her yesterday, just busier, louder, a bit more hectic. We were, after all, in the war zone, if you will, inside this raucous, overcrowded and busy building full of refugees, each one with a story you could probably write a book about.

"Wait here for a moment and let me see if he is here," she said to me. I nodded to her. Where was I going to go anyways, I thought to myself. Home? Home was no longer home, the city life I had grown tired of and wished to escape like so many of us. What the hell was I doing here though? Maybe I would go to Nepal, become a monk, or something, I thought to myself whimsically. I truly believe that every one of us has, at one point or another, had this thought. Leaving life behind and living ascetically amongst nature. I walked forward towards an empty chair, while she walked to the back of the room to converse with someone else.

I sat down, surveying the environment. How do these people work here, experiencing this day in and day out, I thought now? Then again, I thought that about various environments: supermarkets, factories, retail stores, offices. Human beings weren't made to work in such constructs I thought, even though I worked in a cubicle in a skyscraper for years. How I regret those years. You can get back money, you can get back almost anything, but you can't get back time and missed opportunities.

I looked at her again, this young woman who had woken my heart from its slumber. She exuded calm, peace, even happiness in the midst of this madness. She was no human, she was an angel. I was totally mesmerized by her, I confessed this to myself. I realized that I hadn't thought about Anastasya the last couple of days, which I found interesting. Had I forgotten her so quickly? Are we that replaceable? Is there always someone better, as many people are fond of saying? It was all too much to think about. I was enervated and in a place I knew not how to be in.

I noticed an older man entering the room suddenly, and our eyes crossed for a brief second as he walked past me. My jaw dropped. My eyes spread wide open in shock. My heart sank like an anchor which had just been dropped off a major ship, paralyzing the vessel to which it was tied. Absolute fear and dread washed over me like a rainstorm. I became utterly petrified. I stared at him, unable to move anything but my eyes, which were focused squarely on him as he crossed the room slowly. Without a doubt it was him. Much older, more frail, but undeniably him. I could not believe he was still here, so many years later. I would never forget that pointed nose, those hollow brown eyes, that diabolical face. I never forgot what he did to me 23 years ago. I recalled it vividly now just as if it had happened yesterday.

I was seven years old. Always an errant, adventurous child, I liked going where I was not supposed to. It was a warm, sunny day, and I had left the kids and the camp behind and walked down a dusty street towards an older, empty building that had always fascinated me. I never realized that I was being followed. I would have never gone off on my own if I had known what was going to befall me that day. I reached the building area where the pavement had stopped and the road become unruly, but I continued. I climbed over a makeshift wall of rocks that was perhaps two or three feet tall and made my way around to the back of the building. The sun was at its highest point, forcing a sweat. It was eerily silent here, a ways away from the camp.

Unable to find an opening, I thought about heading back, but I noticed a corner of the wall that contained an opening. It was just large enough for me to slip through. The interior of the building wasn't any more interesting than its exterior. Run down, it had large, thick pillars, broken windows and remnants of old machinery and furniture, completely covered with dust and soot. I looked around for a few moments, but quickly became bored and began to worry that someone was looking for me, so I decided to head back. Slipping through the opening again once more, I emerged on the other side, but to my surprise, I was no longer alone. I stood still, staring at one of the officers from the camps. He stared at me, an empty, cold look on his face.

"Far from the camp, aren't you, boy," he said to me, his voice sharp and protracted. He had dark hair, thick brows, and a deep and dark brown pair of eyes and a pointy nose. Nothing about him much stood out, except his nose and his eyes. I will never forget those eyes. He was accompanied by two other young men, certainly younger than him, maybe in their late teens or 20s. Both of them stood in place, flanking the officer on either side. They knew what I was about to endure, though I did not. The officer approached me as I stood still, tense, unsure as to what was happening. What did I know about anything?

He got quite close to me. "You shouldn't have ventured this far, little boy." Turning around to one of the two young boys behind him, he muttered something to them in a gruntled voice. I couldn't make it out, but I believe he said for them to keep an eye out for anyone.

95

Still confused, but frightened as well, I thought about running, but I couldn't quite move. My tiny legs felt paralysed and were buckling with trepidation. He continued staring at me, an arm's length away, looking completely sinister as he clenched his jaw, causing a twitch in his muscle cheeks which I noticed.

I finally managed to twist my legs and spring them forward to the side to run, but by now, I was simply too late, as he grabbed me by my shirt collar, pulling me back, his strength overwhelming my small frame.

"Help, somebody help me!"

That was all I was able to shout before he placed his large right hand over my mouth, wrapped me around his left arm, and lifted me and dragged me to the very corner of the building, not far from the hole, where there was a large rock. He threw me on it with my chest rather hard as I became winded. Unable to breathe clearly, nor scream, I was terrified and confused about what was happening to me.

"Let me go! Let me go!" I begged and screamed. He reached around and placed his hand over my mouth once more. He used his other hand to undress me. I fought him off as best as I could, kicking and trying to shift my frame, but I was just a little boy, I couldn't fight off my own nightmares. Continuing to struggle, exhaustion began to set in and I slowly lost the battle. He did the sordid deed. I struggled for the grueling and painful 5-6 minutes it went on for, but it was in vain. I wasn't sure of how to make sense of what was happening to me, but it felt as though the world was ending and that I was about to die.

I recall thinking about my mother throughout it, wishing more than anything that she was there to help me. On a few occasions, during when I would turn to my right, I noticed that one of the other two behind us merely stood by and watched callously. When the ordeal finally ended, I was absolutely exhausted and in quite a good amount of pain, mentally and physically. I lay still like a fish that had been out of water for too long. My innocence had been stolen from me. I was no longer even crying. I was simply in a state of shock.

"That should teach you not to venture where you aren't supposed to," were his final words to me. They would echo forever in my mind, along with the memory of it. If childhood is paradise, paradise was now lost. I was seven years old.

"Hello, Moshe? Please, wake up!" I heard faintly. I slowly began to come to and noticed Kanda in front of me now, staring into my eyes, knelt down with her hands on my left leg, shaking me. I supposed there were worse ways to be woken. Rolling my eyes and blinking several times as if waking up from a sleep, I opened my eyes fully, my body jerking a few times as I snapped out of what I quickly realized was an incredibly intense and traumatic flashback. My whole body was shaking, and she could see this and was obviously quite concerned and worried. Her face was different, eyes alert, mouth slightly open, skin slightly pale.

"Here, drink this," she said as she passed me a glass of water, which I could scant look at and barely drink. I pushed it away.

"Are you alright? What happened?"

What was I going to say to her, that the monster who had raped me and ruined my life, stolen my innocence and peace from me more than two decades ago, was standing in the same room as us? I remembered that he had walked in, sending me into this tailspin. I looked to my right now, down towards the end of the room to see him there again, seated and doing something on his computer, seemingly not concerned at all with my state. The very sight of him made me begin to panic and heave again. I quickly stood up to flee, but she stopped me.

"Hey!" she yelled, "What's wrong? Please, you're worrying me."

I looked at her for a moment, her beautiful face, her calm voice, her soft touch. "I'm sorry, this was a bad idea, Kanda," I said to her. "I'm really sorry. I have to go."

I looked for my bag. Grabbing it, I walked quickly out of the room. I began pacing quicker down the hallway, only to hear her approach me from behind and grab my right shoulder to stop me in the most delicate manner.

"What the hell is going on here?" she said to me with genuine confusion as she thrust her hands to her sides, frustrated, revealing that she too was indeed human. After all, we are all human, all too human. "Please," she said, imploring. "Tell me, what is the matter?"

I loathed myself at that moment for being there and in this position to begin with. What had I been thinking about this all anyways?

"Listen," I said, "I'm not sure what to tell you, but this was a bad idea."

She stared at me without saying a word, but it was a different woman than the one who I had met yesterday and had encountered today. She had dropped her guard now; she was forced to after what happened.

"Please, I have to go. I don't feel well."

She looked at me. "Okay, I will walk you out at least," she said.

"No!" I yelled back, startling her. "I'm sorry," I said, feeling bad. Reaching out, I grabbed her hands, looking at them closely for the first time, then her eyes, holding her hands all the while. "I'm sorry. I will explain another time. I just have to go now. Please try to understand."

She could see how serious I was. She nodded her head. I couldn't quite release her hands, and it was rather strange anyhow how I held them. Don't we act differently in moments of truth, more genuinely, more affectionately and physically? I finally released them with the reluctance that an idealist does their beliefs.

"Hold on, please," she said rather expressively as she grabbed a pen and pad and wrote her number for me on the back of a slip of paper from her pocket. "Call me if you need anything."

I loathed myself again, but I smiled. I smiled for her, for this stranger I was so drawn to. We both stood there, staring at one another in silence for a moment. I finally turned around and began walking towards the exit, all the while dearly wanting to turn around and look at her once more. I had pursued my past knowing that it would not be easy, hoping that I could confront it. Clearly I could not. Sometimes the past can be more powerful than the present. Like a rock, which thrown into a lake, creates ripples that move outward, so too with the past. An incident from many years ago can continue to ripple forward uninterrupted into the future, its effects continuing to leave imprints in the lake of life.

Chapter 7:
Vengeance

No stranger to long nights, last night may have been my longest. Seeing my childhood rapist had completely shattered me. Whenever I would close my eyes, his face appeared. I kept them open all night; I barely slept. He had aged significantly, not only from time, but perhaps also from the guilt of his actions. Certainly I wasn't the only victim of this cowardly and deplorable man who had robbed me of my innocence as a child. I loathed him with a vengeance.

Kanda, however, I felt something entirely different towards her. She dropped her guard at my sight yesterday, I recalled, revealing to me just how much empathy lay in her heart, how much understanding. I could see it in her eyes, and she could see it in mine. We were both naked for a brief moment, our souls exposed. Was this love? My thoughts soured quickly as he appeared once more. A general malaise and sickness permeated me about it all. I was actually trembling.

Luckily, my uncle had come home very late last night and I managed to avoid him. He certainly would have noticed something was wrong. My aunt, she was easier to convince. I told her I thought I was getting sick, and two hours later, she had brought down homemade chicken soup, God bless her soul.

The truth was that I was enraged that this man was still alive, still at the camps, and still had not been brought to justice after so many years and God knows how many more victims. Banging my fists against my head repeatedly at these thoughts, in agony about it all, I couldn't fight my tears.

"Why, why, why?" I shouted at myself as if someone was there to answer me. Looking at the coffee table in front of me, I noticed the folders with some of their contents out. I reached forward and swiped at them violently with my right hand, knocking them off the table and onto the ground. I yelled certain expletives, at myself, at my father, at life. No one knows what life is. We just live it, long and well if we are lucky.

I made my way over to the washroom and looked at myself in the mirror before bending over and vomiting into the sink. Running the faucet, I soaked my face and I stared at it. How often do we actually look at ourselves in the mirror? Really and truly look at our own face, into our own eyes?

"You're cursed, you're damned and cursed." I repeated bringing back my tears, barely able to recognize myself anymore. "What's the point, man?"

I became still after uttering these words. They resonated with me deeply as I continued staring at myself with a blank expression.

"Just do it already."

Do what, I thought now? Was I talking to myself? I closed my eyes for a moment, feeling as though I was completely losing it. I saw him again and I opened them immediately, enraged, slamming my hand on the sink, yelling once again in frustration. I reached for the biggest bottle of pills I could find in the cabinet. Staring at it, I collapsed to the floor, my back against the wall. I felt completely hopeless, mentally and physically numb. Paralysed, I sat staring at this bottle as if it was salvation. It was not for salvation lies within.

I was terrified and searched for anything to dissuade me and give me strength to redirect my course. I pulled up my shirt, revealing a tattoo I had of each one of my family member's name on my right torso in Farsi. I stared at it. The first one was of my mother. How could I do this to her, to my siblings? In a split-second decision, I threw the bottle at the wall, shattering it and spreading the little white pills all over the washroom like shrapnel. Exhausted, I pulled myself up and forced myself outside for air.

An overcast day, I stepped into the backyard. The weather today was cooler than in previous ones. Closing my eyes, I inhaled a few deep breaths. I couldn't hold it in, however, as I saw him again, that son of a bitch. He was haunting me, this many years later. It enraged me that he was free and still working there. Clenching my teeth at this moment, I cocked my fist and went to punch the sliding glass doors, but luckily stopped. I reached for a cigarette, lighting it up and blowing the smoke into the air.

I had an epiphany of sorts at just that moment, as I was wondering why there was no justice in the world, as if jungles were supposed to have laws. I would punish him myself, I decided then and there in a split second of lucidity and boldness. I had stopped crying and began to feel some calm. An inner voice spoke to me: "He should die, you should do it." Why do we suffer so readily for other people's sins? I had swung the spectrum from anguish and overwhelmed to a resolute vigilante, and I was resolved on killing this man. Uncle Ammad owned a gun, I knew that. I would find it, I convinced myself. I will find the gun and I will kill my rapist.

It was just past noon when I finally stepped outside and made my way to the camps. I had promised my uncle and my aunt that I would stay home today and rest, catch up on some work. Obviously I would not. I had found Uncle Ammad's gun, an old five-chamber pistol, fully loaded, much easier than I had expected. I felt horrible looking around their master bedroom, eventually finding it quite simply on the bottom drawer of his office desk in an unlocked compartment. My resolve aside, I was still a nervous wreck and had already taken two clonazepams today and felt a bit lightheaded. Don't we love and abuse medication for this reason nowadays, to feel just slightly different than normal?

I had searched for the nearest car rental facility around where my uncle lived and took a cab over. I rented the smallest vehicle they had; I had no use for anything larger or more noticeable. Using GPS, though, I still got lost a couple of times, I arrived near the general area of the camps where my uncle had dropped me off the previous two days about an hour later. I parked further back of course, and after many moments of hesitation, I finally stepped out of the vehicle and walked to a rundown and graffiti covered telephone booth, taking out some change and Kanda's number on the slip she had given me. Feeling nervous calling her in this state, I had no choice. Regrettably, she was going to be an indirect accomplice to this act. There is always collateral damage where death is concerned.

Upon hearing the first ring, I abruptly hung up the phone and became nervous and unsure. "Shit" I said out loudly. What if I got caught? My life would be over; my family would be devastated. "No, God damn it" I said, slamming the phone on its base. "You have to do this!" I commanded myself. It was the only way to move forward. For all I knew, he was still raping children, maybe Shuaib, the young boy I had met yesterday. . "Be strong, you can do this. You have to!" I repeated.

I called her again and waited.

"Hello."

Hesitating slightly, she repeated herself and I finally spoke.

"Hi, Kanda."

There was a slight pause, after which she responded affably, "Hello, Moshe." She didn't seem happy to hear from me, I thought.

"I wanted to call and apologize about yesterday."

"Thank you," she responded. "I've been worried about you."

"Yes, well, I don't know what happened, I'm really sorry," I said to her.

"Please don't be. I'm glad you called. How are you now?" she asked.

"I'm better," I lied. "This is all harder for me than I imagined."

"Don't be so hard on yourself," she said. "You wouldn't be human if you didn't react."

If she only knew why I reacted as I did. Her understanding was endearing and brought the first smile of the day to my face.

"Thank you," I said.

"You're welcome."

There was a pause, during which neither of us said anything.

"Look," I finally spoke, cutting the tension, "maybe I could meet you later on, for a coffee, outside the camps?"

"Umm, yeah, sure," she agreed.

"Great. What time do staff members get off usually?"

"Well, it varies," she responded, "but the main day staff, typically around 6 p.m." Closer to evening, that worked, I thought. "I could meet you wherever you like."

I had no intention of actually meeting her, sadly. Here I was, manipulating another girl, I caught myself thinking.

"Sure, that could work. How about I call you around 5:30 p.m. and we can firm things up then?"

She agreed and we said our goodbyes. Poor girl, she didn't deserve to be a pawn in this game, but I had no choice. We're all pawns in other people's lives at some point or another.

It dawned upon me that I really hadn't planned this out. If the son of a bitch didn't leave around the same time, or exit using the front gates, I had no chance of following him. I didn't have many options. I had to rely on hope and luck.

I had a few hours. I decided to drive down towards the Bosphorous River near the Blue Mosque where me and uncle had been two nights ago. Istanbul is an undeniable city. It's a mix of the old and the new, and it's beautiful, especially the old parts. It was a city nonetheless, filled with millions scurrying about like ants building a great mound. What of all this toil and effort and labour we embark upon everyday? What is it all for?

I shook off the thought; this was no time for philosophical reflection. I had something important to accomplish. Time seemed to move achingly slow. The sun was past its zenith for the day, but shined brightly for me as I stood near the water again, sitting on a bench people watching, that old pastime of our species that we all love to do. Why are we drawn to observing others so often? It seems today all we do is compare ourselves to them. Are we not self-sufficient anymore? I had always gathered that we watch others because we see in them ourselves, past or present, actual or potential. Nevertheless, what the hell are we all here for anyways, I thought to myself now? No one really knows; I certainly didn't. This was no time for meditating on life's eternal questions. I looked at my watch. It was time to start driving back to the camps.

It was just before 6 p.m. Parking discreetly on the opposite road, behind a few cars and the cover of a tree, I had a direct line of sight on the compound's main entrance. People slowly started to come out, but not him yet. It was just past 630 p.m. when Kanda finally emerged and started walking in the direction of the major car park down the street to her left and out of sight from me. I felt bad that I had lied to her and left her hanging. I wish I could just follow her instead, but right now, I knew what I was here to do and I kept looking out for my target.

It was nearly 7 p.m. and doubt and a sense of defeat were beginning to set in. My patience was finally rewarded, however, as he emerged. I sat up and became poised quickly. Crossing the street, he sat at a bus shelter. He walked rather slowly, revealing his age, which I hadn't quite noticed yesterday. The weight of the impending deed was heavy; my breathing conveyed this. Turning on the engine, I waited for the bus to arrive. Checking the glove compartment, the gun was still there, in between a pink newspaper. The sight of it still shook me, and I couldn't take my eyes off it. Just then, the bus arrived. Slamming the compartment shut finally, I pulled out and in pursuit.

It wasn't easy following this vehicle in a city you aren't familiar with. I remained vigilant, however, following it directly from behind for almost 20 minutes towards the old port, a lower class area, where he finally got off. Unsure as to what to do next to avoid drawing attention, I simply stayed put. Luckily, there were no cars behind me. Observing from afar, he had crossed the street and was opening the door to a building and disappeared behind it. I thought about stepping out to follow, but hesitated. I kept my eyes on this building for any sign that might indicate which apartment was his. After a few moments, the apartment lights turned on in a second-floor apartment facing the street. The curtains were pulled next, and I could see him again, this rapist, this dead man. It was becoming dark. The streets light came on. Sitting precariously on the side of the road, I drove ahead down the street further to look for a more suitable spot to park the vehicle. Well, out of sight, but not too far to reach in a hurry.

I had parked and began to feel the imminence and weight of what was before me. Nervous, I was smoking a cigarette, the vapours swirling in front of me like some mystic spirit. I kept looking at my mirrors to see if anyone was around. It was a rather quiet street, save for the odd car that passed every few minutes.

I looked at my phone and saw a missed call from my uncle. "Shit" I said to myself. I responded by sending him a text message and telling him that I needed some air and had come downtown for some sightseeing. I turned off the phone and put it away.

Opening the glove compartment, I grabbed the newspaper and pulled it out. Looking around once more in all directions, not seeing anyone, I pulled out the stainless steel gun and stared at it. I picked it up with my right hand, gently as if it was some sleeping animal I did not want to wake.

My hands were trembling. "Damn it" I exclaimed, "how am I supposed to shoot someone like this?" I tried not to think about it, putting the gun between my legs, closing my eyes, and trying to calm down. I think I prayed at that moment. I'm not sure to whom or what, but I prayed.

The street lamps were few and far in between, creating dark patches on the street in which one could hide. I neared his apartment on foot, the gun in my pocket. I had the fear of life in me, but there was no turning back. My senses were elevated because of the adrenaline pumping through my veins. I could actually feel and hear my heartbeat. I neared his apartment, noticing that his light was still on.

Just then, I heard a noise to my left which startled me. Turning immediately, I couldn't see anything. A drop of sweat fell on my cheek from just above my right brow. Placing my hand there, I felt just how much I was perspiring. I heard the noise once more and jumped around again, but this time, was dismayed by a rather burly and unkempt man, approaching me with a metal bar in his hand. Shocked, I turned to face him directly, my back facing the apartment. To my dismay, another man appeared from my right, taller, more slender, but equally malicious looking. I continued pacing back slowly onto the curb.

"You're in the wrong part of town," the shorter one finally said to me with a grin, revealing his rotting teeth. I looked him in the eyes, then at his hand containing the metal bar.

"Look," I said, "I'm just a tourist and I'm leaving town tomorrow. I can offer you the cash in my pocket and we can go our own ways."

They paced a couple steps towards me without responding. I could feel my heart moving up my throat, thumping rapidly, like a deep, hollow drum.

"Stay back," I yelled, feeling endangered. "I have a weapon."

Neither seemed to care, if they believed me to begin with. I pulled out my wallet, gently holding it in the air.

"Just take it and be gone, please," I implored them. The shorter one said something in Turkish to me as his glance went cold and he stepped forward, quickly forcing me to react and pull out my gun, which I pointed directly at him. He was caught off guard by this; I could tell from the expression on his face. It had gone from looking like a snickering wolf to a rattled one.

Everyone stood still, unflinching. Finally, he began laughing, utterly confounding me. He said something to his partner, who also began to laugh lightly as he looked back at me. They stepped forward a few feet. I stood still, paralysed, but still pointing the gun. I realized why they laughed. My hands, they were shaking. Walking towards me now more confidently, he placed his right hand on the gun, easily pulling it from me and throwing it to his friend who caught it. I was horrified, I couldn't move. A second later, I felt a heavy blow to my face. I fell back, onto the ground. Disoriented and in shock, I noticed him coming in now, grabbing me by my shirt, lifting me up slightly, then punching me again. I feared for my life, knowing I could easily be beaten and shot by these guys.

As he went in for a third swing, I threw up my arms in defence and turned my face away, but then heard the door behind me swing open and someone yell in Turkish, an old man. The thug relinquished his hold on me then, standing up erect and retreating, a look on his face composed of shock and worry. I dropped my head on the cement, disoriented, but trying to catch my breath and refocus my vision, which was blurry. I slowly sat up, feeling dizzy and nauseous. I spat on the ground ahead of me, a thick wad of blood and saliva. I was bleeding quite badly as I touched my eye and mouth areas.

I finally turned around to see who it was that had interjected, likely saving my life. My face froze immediately. It was none other than him, my rapist, holding a large double barrel shotgun pointed at the thugs. They say truth is stranger than fiction. Reality certainly seemed to be.

Unable to take my eyes off him, I wasn't sure how to react, how to feel. He spoke to the thugs in Turkish, in a deep, raspy drawl, prompting them to walk back after the one had slid my uncle's gun back over towards me. Eventually, they turned around and began to run away. I felt an incredible relief at seeing them vanish from sight, but then anxiety, as I looked back at my rapist with whom I remained.

He finally looked down at me. "You're okay?" he asked.

I simply nodded, staring without blinking. He tiptoed over and picked up my uncle's gun, making me quite nervous. He stared at me, then turned around and walked back to his building, opening the door and uttering "come in," as it closed behind him. Such a scenario is the stuff bizarre dreams are made of. This, however, was reality. It was all happening. I slowly stood up and made my way to the door which he had left open for me.

I caught up with him at the top of the stairs of this dingy and dark old building. He continued to walk towards his apartment, opening the creaky green door and walking in without turning to look at me. Was I actually going to enter his home? Taking a few steps forward, I deliberated about this, but realized I had come too far to turn around, and I needed uncle's gun back. I stepped into his apartment. As I did, I noticed him placing his shotgun beside the couch. I looked at him up close for the first time as he turned around. I saw before me only the shadow of a man, nothing more. Don't people always look dramatically different when you get up close to them?

He was a frail man, weathered and seemingly sick as he coughed steadily. I noticed a bouquet of pills on his coffee table. Everywhere in sight, there were stacks of newspapers and boxes. He was clearly a hoarder. The whole place smelled rather dank and stale and was poorly lit. It smelled like the prelude to death.

"Come with me, boy," he said as he walked past me and up the hallway. My eyes followed him like a dog does his master. I felt as though I was witnessing a ghost.

"You need to wash and disinfect that," he said as he turned into a room, I presumed the washroom. I gingerly walked up the hallway, feeling incredibly odd about this all. Stepping into the dimly lit bathroom, he got out of my way. Looking into the mirror, I noticed how badly bruised my face was. How would I explain this to uncle and aunt? He put down a brown bottle on the counter and walked away, asking me if I wanted a drink. I needed one.

In the living room, I was wracked by my indecision. Does one good deed cancel out a bad one? Did I owe this man anything, mercy? "No, no," I whispered to myself. What he had done to me and put me through all these years, that was wrong and he deserved to die for it. I felt resolute again, realizing his shotgun was nearby as I scoured for it and noticed it to my right by the lamp table. I looked back at him, and then took a few steps towards it.

"This neighbourhood used to be safe," he said now, "but ever since all the immigrants came in and took the jobs, it's become a dangerous place, even for an old man like me." He turned around with two drinks in his hand and proceeded to walk out of the kitchen. I released my grip on his shotgun and stepped forward as he walked back into the living room and brought me something that resembled scotch in some old, dirty glass. I don't think he had noticed my movements.

"Here, take this, it will help numb the pain." I stared at the glass, downing it in one gulp. It was cheap scotch. "Another one?"

I nodded my head in agreement, avoiding looking at him so as to avoid feeling pity. It's much easier to hurt people when you aren't looking at them.

"In the kitchen, go ahead," he said as he walked over to the couch and sat down, grimacing as he bent over, apparently in pain. I looked at him, but not for long. My eyes wouldn't bear it. I walked over to the kitchen and poured another glass, looking at him again from the opening in the wall. I noticed knives in front of me. One of them would do, and it would be quieter than a gun, I thought. I went for one, but was interrupted by him again, recoiling my hand.

"Life moves fast, you're old and useless before you know it. Even sitting down can be painful," he muttered.

"You shouldn't have lived this long," I said quietly. What did he know about pain?

"What are you doing in Turkey?" he asked me. "What are you doing in this neighbourhood of all places?"

I wasn't sure what to say. I downed my drink quickly, poured another one, and left the kitchen, a small knife tucked in my pocket.

"I'm just visiting. I got lost," I said.

He turned on the TV. "I have spent all my life here. I'll die here too. Hopefully soon."

His last words, hopefully soon, what did he mean by that? Was he contrite about his sins? Perhaps this was all meant to be, tonight's events. Everything does after all happen for a reason. Just then, he began coughing repeatedly, almost as if he was choking.

"Puffer," he said in between coughs and pointing in my direction, "pass it to me."

I looked down at the lamp table to my left and noticed it. His coughing worsened. He couldn't talk anymore, but kept pointing to it as he bent over practically choking. A part of me relished seeing him in this state. I simply looked upon him, then at the puffer, but did not move.

"Please!" I could hear him grunt out, looking down at the ground. I felt uncomfortable and thought about leaving, taking a few steps towards the door. I couldn't do it.

"God damn it," I said quietly. Two wrongs never make a right. I stepped back and retrieved his puffer, handing it over to him. He desperately took a few botched inhales and finally calmed himself down. Slinking back into his couch, he fought to regain his breath. He was a worn-out man, his face quite wrinkled, his eyes hollow like a dried-up well, his teeth ragged and yellow. His hair had thinned significantly, and what he had left was slicked back straight, ghost white. I could have gotten him some water, perhaps, but it was enough that I wasn't going to let him suffocate anymore, I thought. I loathed this whole situation and everything about it.

He was finally looking at me, but in an eerily expressionless manner. My rage had abated, but it was still within me. I felt it briefly for an instant, wanting to lunge at him and choke him myself with my bare hands, but I could not. This man was already dead.

I made my way for the door, grabbing the handle, but I was immediately stopped by something he said.

"Don't forget your gun, boy."

I turned around to look at him, my face the look of shock as my eyes widened open and he reached into his pant pocket and pulled out my gun. Holding it in his hand, which was resting on his leg, it was pointed at me, fully loaded; shivers slid down my spine. There was a strange look on his face. Did he know after all? Was he aware when I refused to hand him his puffer? I stood still, petrified, unsure as to what to do. I finally walked over to him tepidly, grabbing it from his leg. He was no longer looking at me, but ahead, a dead expression on his face, soulless. I had my chance yet again to kill him, to seek my vengeance on this man who had taken something from me I would never get back. I could not do it however. He seemed to be suffering enough as it was. It is not our place to play judge or jury. Life does that well itself.

Regardless, I had made up my mind already. Someone I loved once told me that the right thing to do is usually the hard thing to do. I wanted to put a bullet through this man's head, but that would only be putting one through mine. I would forgive him his trespass towards me. I placed the gun in my pocket and took out the knife and put it on the table. He didn't notice this.

"Thank you for helping me tonight," I said. No response. Walking back to the door, opening it, taking one step forward towards the hallway, I stopped. Turning back, I took one last look at this sick, lonely, tormented old man. I tried to make peace with this all, knowing that I would never see him again. I finally closed the door, pulling it slowly and seeing him fade from sight. I walked down the barely lit stairs, which creaked with every step, and onto the dark street. I had never spared a life, nor forgiven someone to that extent before. It felt different. I felt different. I got into the car and drove off into the night. I felt better already. Nothing is heavier than hatred and anger. Nothing is lighter than love and peace.

Chapter 8:
New Hope

"Wake up!"

Startled like a sleeping bird whose nest is shaken by prey, I opened my eyes to see Uncle Ammad staring at me. His eyes were wide open with concern as he knelt beside me on the couch.

"It's important you are awake right now. I'm not sure if you are suffering from a concussion or not."

Disoriented, I quickly realized it was morning, but my thoughts returned to the previous night.

Last night, after I got home, uncle had caught me sneaking in, despite my attempts to enter unnoticed. It was quite late and he had waited up for me out of worry. He gasped upon seeing my face up close. Bloodied and cut, my head swollen, my clothing torn and sullied with blood and dirt, how could I blame him?

Unfortunately, our interaction and noise also woke Aunt Gelareh. I was upset with myself for allowing this all to happen. She had come running down the stairs, groggy eyed, dithering in her usual clumsy manner, a ridiculous purple robe covering her, uttering my name repeatedly while fumbling to get her thick glasses on. Noticing my face as she neared the end of the stairway, she nearly slipped and fell on the last step, catching herself by the guardrail. If it wasn't for the solemn nature of the moment, I would have fallen over with laughter at her sight. Such a kind, but clumsy soul. Don't all clumsy people have gentle souls?

Nothing about any of this was funny, however. Initially, I told them that I had been mugged and fought back. I knew I could convince my aunt, but not my uncle. I did my best to alleviate her worries for now and asked her for some tea and ice, which she quickly tended to.

"Please," I implored Uncle Ammad, looking over his shoulder to make sure she was gone, "ensure she goes back to sleep and I will tell you everything." Looking at me aghast, shaking his head and clearly troubled by my state, he promised he would do so.

Aunt Gelareh returned a few moments later with the items. She insisted on applying the ice herself.

"Your hands will get cold and numb. You just rest now."

"Auntie, I'll be fine. I'd prefer to just lie down and sleep it off, thank you."

"Oh, oh, okay," she squealed, a nervous expression forming on her face as she clearly felt helpless. "Well, drink your tea then, at least."

Doing so to appease her, I threw my uncle a glance while she wasn't looking. He got the message. He convinced her to retire and promised he would be up shortly. She reluctantly agreed, cursing my muggers as she kissed me on the forehead and went back upstairs, muttering something along the way, talking to herself.

With her out of sight, uncle and I talked for a couple hours. I told him everything, not only of the night, but also of the rape. I didn't reveal my intention of killing my rapist, however, just that I wanted to confront him. His blank stare and lack of response spoke volumes. He never even once made a joke or a smart quip during the whole time we talked, rare for him. His only insistence was that we visit the emergency room.

"Cuts and bumps," I responded, "they will heal, Uncle." It's the mental wounds that linger long after such ordeals. Spirit is more sensitive than flesh.

"Listen," he said, "I am responsible for you here. You can't expect me to just sit still and not do anything when I see you like this."

I was in no arguing mood. "I am fine, uncle," I responded with more force, catching him off guard. Staring at one another for a moment, I dropped my head, feeling dejected, and asked him to let me be. I promised him I would sleep.

Snapping out of my recollection of last night, I sat up on the couch and my uncle looked at me as if I was some alien.

"I'm alright, you know," I said. That was a lie. It was a new day at least, and with it, a new hope, but something still felt unfulfilling about life. I wondered what I would do, what my next step would be. Yes, I had confronted one of my oldest demons and horrendous episodes of my past by confronting my rapist. Even so, I still wasn't quite ready to return home just yet, to return to nothing. I had looked a bit further into my father's files last night after uncle had finally retired to bed. I had come across a certain interesting passage in which my father spoke of a great guilt for "leaving them behind." Leave who behind, I kept thinking now? I also came across yet another picture of the young girl and also the veiled woman. Who the hell are they?

"Please drink this," my uncle said, disrupting my train of thought as he had gone and brought me a glass of fresh juice and an Advil. "I certainly hope you will leave everything be now. This whole idea of visiting the camps was not good for you." He had a dejected look on his face, pointing to mine and shaking his head in regret as if he was responsible.

"Uncle, I did this myself, not you."

He continued to stare at me. "So what now, young man?"

I sipped the juice and swallowed the Advil. "Well, I need to learn more about this all," I said as I lifted up my father's notepad and the picture of the child and women. I had told uncle about father's files last night, but he was actually seeing them now. He browsed through it quickly, taking a long look at both pictures.

"Who are they?" he finally said to me, continuing to stare at them.

"I'm not sure, but I would like to find out."

He looked up at me, placing the items on the table. "And how do you plan on doing that, Sherlock?" The truth is that I didn't quite know and had only one idea. "Well," he said, eager for a response.

"Do you remember father's best friend and his colleague from the newspaper, Riazi?"

His face became stiff. "Surely you aren't thinking what I think you're thinking?"

In fact, I was. My options were slim. Who else would know the details of my father's life intimately?

"If anyone might know anything about any of this stuff here, it's going to be someone who was close to father from the very beginning, someone who knew him well, who he shared information with."

His eyes furrowed, and he looked away in displeasure.

"He trusted Riazi unequivocally, did he not?"

I knew this because he was one of the few people my father actually kept in touch with while I was growing up, and I recalled their incredible kinship during our time in Turkey. They had even spent time in prison together in Tehran. My uncle did not seem pleased talking about him and promised me he knew nothing more about it all: the child, the woman, the items in the notebooks. I believed him. He wouldn't lie to me. Would he?

"So you know nothing about him, or where he might be?" I pressed. He remained quiet, but his expression spoke loudly. "Uncle, please, don't make me have to beg you."

"Damn, it boy, why can't you just let it go already, what will any of this achieve?" he yelled. He was clearly upset as he stood up and paced a few steps forward, one hand on his hip, the other on his face.

"Uncle Ammad," I said, standing up to face him, "please, this is my life here, I have to know. I've come this far already."

After a pause, he mumbled something I could not quite make out.

"Excuse me? I didn't quite hear you, uncle," I said.

"Kiev, Ukraine!" he shouted loudly as he turned around to face me. Ukraine wasn't all that far and certainly accessible from Turkey. I felt hopeful again for a moment. Of course, I had to find him first and ensure he would talk to me, but that seemed secondary.

"Riazi is in Kiev?" I asked to confirm. "How do you know this? Are you two friends?"

"No, we're not friends. That man doesn't have friends," he said as he walked back past me. "He helped me with some business on a few occasions. I've helped him by taking some items back to Iran for him, given that he cannot return. We keep in touch."

Great, I thought, as a smile formed on my face. I immediately asked my uncle to make contact with him and to arrange for us to meet in Kiev. I had always wanted to visit this old and historic city anyways. What better time than now while I was already on this journey and so close by? Ukraine was only a couple hours flight away after all.

"I don't like this at all," he said. "I said the same thing about the camps and I was right. And believe me, Riazi is no cupcake, he may not even talk to you."

Of course he would talk to me, I thought. I was his deceased best friend's son. There are codes of conduct after all amongst men, especially with the older generation.

"Uncle," I said curtly as I put up my right hand in a stopping gesture, "please, don't argue with me and just do it."

He reluctantly agreed and promised me that he would. He was wrong about the camps too. I hadn't told him about Kanda. Meeting her alone was worth all the trouble I had to endure. Something about her resonated deeply with my heart.

"Hello." It was that soft voice again, it washed over me comfortingly like dew over leaves. "Hello?" she said again into the phone.

"Say something, you idiot," I thought to myself. "Hi, Kanda," I finally managed to utter.

"Oh, hello," she said, sounding surprised to hear from me. "What happened to you yesterday? I waited for you to call me for quite a while you know."

I couldn't quite tell her what had happened obviously. "I'm sorry, I actually got into an altercation by the water. I'm a bit roughed up." Her voice dried up and the tone changed immediately.

"What do you mean altercation? During the day? Are you alright?"

"Yes," I responded, "some bruises and cuts, but I'm fine."

"Oh my goodness."

We both went quiet for a moment.

"Listen, I'm not going to be returning to the camps anymore," I said. "It's all really harder than I imagined."

"Well," she said, "that's understandable, but didn't you want to speak with the case officer from your time here?" She obviously did not know that I already had in the most dramatic of fashions just last night.

"No, that won't be necessary anymore," I said.

"Okay," she responded, sounding confused, her voice broken.

"Listen," I said, "I was hoping we could chat briefly today, grab that coffee after all. I may be leaving soon."

"Oh, that's too bad," she responded. "Where are you going?"

"I just need to go visit some old family in Ukraine. I'm leaving tomorrow."

There was a pause.

"I see. Well, that doesn't leave us much time to meet then, does it?" she responded.

Was I being rejected by her?

"Sure, let's meet tonight."

I breathed a sigh of relief, but also sadness at the thought that I was leaving her here. In my haste to seek the truth and head to Kiev, it had not yet fully dawned upon me that I was incredibly attracted and drawn to this young woman. I had second thoughts about leaving her and Turkey. Perhaps Kiev could wait, I thought. Who was I kidding, I couldn't wait any longer. I convinced myself that I could always come back for her. The very thought of sitting across from her, alone, uninterrupted made me happy. We would be meeting by the aquarium near the main bridge. Arrangements were now made.

I walked upstairs and saw Uncle Ammad on his computer at his work table. I made my way quietly to his room to put his gun back. Clearly, he hadn't noticed it was missing. Thank God.

"Uncle," I said, drawing his head up towards me, "I'm heading downtown for a walk now, then meeting someone from the camp for a coffee."

He looked at me askance, but then said, "I'll drive you." I thanked him for the offer, but reminded him that I had to return the rental car and I needed some air and would take public transportation.

"It's quite far," he said.

"I have time. Perhaps you can pick me up later if you're around the area."

He nodded, but looked unhappy and returned to his work.

"Any luck with Riazi yet?" I asked him.

Without turning around, he answered that he had tried, but only got his answering machine. I stood there, staring at him until he finally turned around to face me.

"Once I hear from him, I will let you know. You have your cell, right?"

"Yes, I do."

I made my way out and into the hot Istanbul afternoon. I needed some personal time to digest everything that had happened. I dropped off the rental car and hailed down a taxi. Providing the driver with my destination, I placed my head against the window pane, fatigued and nervous, but excited to be seeing her again.

It was nearly 6 p.m. and I was strolling around the general area of the café we had agreed on when I received a call from Uncle Ammad.

"Hey, uncle."

"Hey, yourself," he responded. "I spoke with him. He is in Kiev."

"And?"

"He was surprised, but said he will meet you if indeed that is what you wish, only because of your father."

I was relieved naturally, but I wasn't sure what to say, I had expected it to be a bit more difficult.

"Wow, that is great, uncle. Thank you."

"Listen," my uncle said, "Riazi is not an easy or pleasant person to deal with. In fact, he is an outright asshole." Uncle was probably trying to scare me into backing out. "He's a rather hard and bitter old man. Don't expect a warm reception of any sort from him." His description seemed to fit the bill. An isolated and broody intellectual who was old and alone, what more could I expect? In fact, it sounded like a description of my father.

"I need something else from you, please?" I asked him.

"What is it? You want me to drive you to Kiev perhaps?"

"Huh, no, not quite," I said. "If I give you my passport and credit card information, can you book me a flight for tomorrow, please?"

"I don't even think you can book for tomorrow this late. I would imagine there aren't too many flights to Kiev daily. It isn't exactly a vacation spot. What's the rush? Why don't you sleep on it tonight, then decide tomorrow?"

A part of me wanted to stay here for now, perhaps get to know her better, but another wanted to continue on with the journey I found myself on. If there was anyone that could shed some light on my father, it was Riazi. I barely recalled him, just sense impressions and faint memories. He was like my father, however, that much I knew or recalled. They were best friends after all. I felt nervous about meeting him and what he might reveal, but I had to do it. As they rightfully say, those who don't study the past are doomed to repeat it. I did not want to become my father, but if I had learned anything on this trip, it was that I didn't know him all that well to begin with.

"Uncle, please just look for me and call me if you find anything." He gave in and promised me that he would.

My thoughts switched over to Kanda completely now. I barely even knew her, but I had a deep affinity to her, that much was obvious. Did she feel anything for me? It didn't matter. Certain people are like magnets in each other's presence. When they are brought together, despite never having met before, they are immediately drawn towards one another by an invisible force. It was as such with us; at least for me and I hoped her too.

It was almost a quarter after six and I was starting to get nervous. "Where is she?" I whispered to myself, nervously looking around the bar to see if I could spot her. Had she changed her mind? Perhaps my rapist did indeed know who I was and had spoken with her today. I shook my head, realizing how ridiculous and farfetched that sounded.

Just then a young server walked by me whom I stopped. "Excuse me." She seemed startled. "I'm sorry, but is this Turkmicha Cafe?"

"Yes" she responded with a blank face.

"There is no other similar bar around here?"

"No, there is not," she responded curtly.

"Thank you," I said to her as she resumed her work. I was in the right place, so where was she? My phone rang just then, exciting me. "Hey." It was my uncle.

"Hey, uncle," I responded back.

"So there are two flights leaving Istanbul tomorrow to Kiev, 1130 a.m. and 4 p.m. It is a four-hour flight. Which would you like?"

Before I could say anything, he continued. "And Riazi will pick you up, but not from the airport. Apparently it is too far from where he lives. You'll have to get into the city yourself."

How far could it be, I thought to myself now? "Ummm, earlier is better," I responded.

A pause ensued.

"Uncle?"

"Yes, I'm here. Are you completely sure about this? There is no rush, you know, Kiev and Riazi aren't going anywhere." He had a point, but I was afraid I might change my mind if I didn't go right away.

"Please book it for me," I said resolutely.

"Alright, as you wish."

Just then, my attention was immediately drawn elsewhere as I saw her come in, clearly hurried, a bit frazzled, but as beautiful as I recalled her. You know those individuals whose energy and essence fills up the space all around them? She was such a person. There was something about Kanda.

"I have to go uncle, please book that flight for me," I said promptly, hanging up the phone without even saying bye.

I felt relieved at her arrival; the mere sight of her made me happy. A wide smile had forced itself upon my face as she eventually saw me, waved, and started walking over. Standing up while she approached me, she stopped in front of me, creating a slightly awkward situation, given that she was looking directly at my bruised face, confused and shocked.

"Oh my God," she exclaimed, placing her right hand over her mouth. "What happened to you?" I looked down and away as if shy, but in fact, just slightly embarrassed. "How did this happen?"

I had to tell her something. "A few guys tried to rough me up for my cash and jewelry and we had a go of it. Really, I'm fine, let's not focus on it."

She sat down. "I'm really very sorry for being late. Istanbul traffic can be impossible sometimes."

Staring at her, she smiled gently, and I witnessed dimples forming at the tips of where her cheeks began. "Are you alright?" she said, catching me drifting.

"Yes," I said, snapping out of it. "Yes, I'm fine. Forgive me."

"Listen," both of us said at almost the same time a few seconds later. We looked at each other and laughed.

"Please," I said to her, "go ahead."

She ran her hand through her hair, delighting me. "I don't want you to feel bad about what happened at the camp the other day. You seemed quite upset at yourself over it." I did not want to recall that incident anymore and told her this. She understood and we dropped it.

We spent the next hour chatting, getting to know more about one another. For the first time in weeks, life felt normal again. I was so completely in the present that the past and future did not seem to exist. She seemed to have that effect on me. Did I induce the same in her?

She was an orphan from a very young age who had never met her biological parents and knew nothing about them. She was adopted by a Turkish couple while still only a few years old. Her mother was a teacher, her father an electrician. She had grown up just outside Istanbul, but spent quite a bit of time in the city until finally relocating here for university, where she completed her degree in social work. She had worked at the camps ever since she graduated three years ago. I found out that she was 27 years old, five years my junior. She struck me as somewhat naïve when she talked about social inequality and politics. She wasn't perfect after all; no one is.

Eventually, she wanted to know more about me, naturally. I told her about the salient points of my life, avoiding my father where possible. I told her just enough, but not too much. Isn't that always best in social matters? I did my best to keep it about her. Her spirit was subtle, but undeniable. At times, I would stare into her eyes and get lost in them, almost as if I knew her. Maybe we were both friends in another life? I believed in them, I think. Don't we all? We've all felt déjà vu after all. How else can you explain déjà vu if not previous lives? I had not delighted so much in listening to someone speak in recent memory as I did listening to her for that hour, or so. It was perfect. Time stood still.

"Kanda," I said, "I need to ask you something that's important."

Her eyes thickened a bit. "What is it?"

Hesitating, I wasn't sure how she would react. I didn't want her to feel as though this was all a ruse to utilize her to my ends. "I need to know if there is any more information about my father that might be contained on file at the camp?"

She sat back and didn't speak. "What do you mean?"

"Well," I responded, "whatever is in the file, I'd like to know it. There must be something more in there considering his profile."

She continued to stare at me, clearly uncomfortable as her eyes kept wandering off mine.

"Look, I'm sorry," I said to her genuinely, "I would never ask you this, but I have no one else to go to. Please, could you help me?"

She faced me, but her warmth had faded. "What you're asking me to do, it's not only illegal, it's not right," she whispered as if someone else was listening.

"I understand that, I do," I said to her, lying partially as I didn't think there was a moral dimension to all this. "No one will know, you have my word."

She said something that hurt me next. "How can I know that? I barely know you. You could be using me for all I know right now."

How could she say that, I thought to myself? I really thought we had a bond after what happened at the camps yesterday. I thought that she had seen the good in me, that she trusted me.

"Look," she said, "I'm sorry, I didn't mean for it to sound like that. I'm sure your intentions are good. I just cannot do this. I just can't. I'm really sorry."

I stormed the table with my fist, landing it hard on the thick wood like a justice does the gavel on its base in court. It was not a premeditated act, I had merely reacted to my emotions.

"Damn your sense of righteousness," I said. She was caught off guard and stunned; she sat there visibly tense and uncomfortable. I closed my eyes for a moment and took a deep breath, regretting my lack of discipline.

"I'm sorry," I said. "I'm not sure what is wrong with me lately. I'm just lost." I had a tone of regret, my voice was lowered, my head down, and my arms crossed on the table. She remained silent. Finally, she placed her right hand on my arms and drew up my face again.

"Perhaps this was a bad idea," I said, looking at her.

"It's fine," she responded. "Let's pretend like it never happened. Don't worry about it."

I felt like a complete idiot. I really thought there was something between us and that she would do this for me. It broke my heart that I was wrong. False hope in love is most disheartening and it happens all too often. I summoned the server over and asked for the bill.

It was a warm, pleasant night. Pacing a few steps up the sidewalk, I was about to say something to her to break the silence when she surprised me by doing so first. She touched my arm and stopped me from walking. We turned, facing each other now.

"I will do it for you," she said.

Unable to speak, I simply stared at her adoringly, a faint smile on my face.

"Thank you."

"Don't thank me yet," she responded. We continued to stare at each other, eyes locked. I grabbed her hand and placed mine on her face, cupping her cheek and caressing it with my thumb. I wanted to kiss her, but I couldn't, it wouldn't have been fair on her. Sometimes in life, not doing something is more meaningful and powerful than doing it. The right thing to do is often the hard thing to do. I relinquished her hand and took my hand off her face, not wanting to ruin whatever it was we had developed in such a short period of time. You ruin a feather by touching it.

"I should go now," she said at this point.

"Yes, you should."

"I have your number. I will let you know," she said. I simply nodded. Turning around, she walked away while I stood still, seeing her drift away like a phantom, down a small hill, and then completely out of sight as she turned right into an alleyway. I stood there the whole time, quietly hoping that she would turn around. She never did. I was happy nonetheless with how it had all gone. Of course, I wanted to know what was in those files, but I felt more drawn to her than to them.

Istanbul hadn't been easy on me; it never seemed to be, but I did not regret coming here. I found out something significant about my father and I faced my biggest and oldest demon. And of course, I met her. Who knew what was to come from all this in time, especially since I was headed even further to Kiev now? Things in life always take time to settle and find their balance. Just as the sound of lighting reverberates across a landscape long after the lightning itself has struck, so it is with revelations of truth and encounters with other souls. Their effects linger and their consequences materialize long after they've occurred.

Chapter 9:
The Revelation

The flight from Istanbul to Kiev took just over four hours. It did not escape me that my father, a staunch and devoted communist, would have loved to visit this place, the birthplace of Russian culture and civilization. Anastasya also had roots here. I thought about her, the first time in a couple of days. Despite what had happened between us, she had still been a part of my life for some time. We all have difficultly letting go of past lovers, and we all struggle with it. Love always lingers, even if it doesn't survive. I no longer felt the same about her however. Nothing felt the same anymore.

Walking through the main airport, it was as drab as I had expected. The large, grey concrete walls were rather bleak and austere. The guards positioned between them, intimidating and cold. I walked steadily past them on my way towards the outside. The language was foreign to me. Everyone seemed rather unhappy, if I could say so, maybe even angry. "What do you expect of a place that is known for its vodka, its endemic corruption, and its bitter cold and brutal history?" I thought to myself.

Riazi had agreed to see me, but he couldn't pick me up from the airport; or wouldn't. Uncle Ammad had warned me about him, describing him as a bitter, old man, a hardcore intellectual like my father who had never gotten married or had kids, who had never recovered from having to flee Iran, and his passion and livelihood, journalism and politics. "Expect little and tread lightly with him," were his exact words of advice for me. Most importantly, this was my father's best friend, his comrade, his closest confidante. This was the man whom I hoped would finally have the answers I was looking for.

Clearing the passport area and picking up the luggage, I purchased a ticket for the bus that would take me to the main thoroughfare of this city, Kreschyatek, where I would be picked up by him at 5 p.m. The ride was a rather bumpy and sobering one, complete in a very old Soviet era bus with ripped seats, a bumpy suspension, and a horrendous blue and steel façade. After what seemed like a very long ride, I arrived at the pickup point in downtown Kiev and disembarked, stepping onto a large pavilion area and right into a crowd of people. Overcome with a unique feeling experienced only by a consummate wanderer and traveler, joy amongst the unknown, I stood still for a moment and closed my eyes to take a deep breath and capture it all. How often do we just stand still, close our eyes, breathe, and capture the moment? Not often enough.

Looking at the clock on one particular building, it was just past our agreed upon pickup time, and I began looking for a grey sedan. There were so many, how the hell was I supposed to know which one was him? Just as I was about to pull out my phone and call Riazi, I heard a couple of honks, which drew my head up and to my right, where there sat parked a grey sedan with its caution lights on. I walked towards it, nervously, nearly running into someone. Did he notice? He had spotted me by the Fedora I was wearing?

I bent down at the passenger window, looking in and seeing a man I did not recognize immediately, even though I had seen his picture. An older man, nearly 70, I had expected an emaciated figure, but here was a robust person with an imposing aura about him. He had a thick, full head of porcelain white hair that was combed back, but quite fluffy. His face wore a scruffy black and pepper beard, bushy white eyebrows, and deep, dark brown eyes behind thick silver spectacles. He came across as a warrior almost. I was frozen, my eyes glued on him, but I finally managed a faint smile to ease the tension and awkwardness. He remained absolutely expressionless, a look as cold as January. He reached over finally and pushed open the door, hitting me as it swung, snapping me out of my stare. Startled, I pulled the door open and sat inside the car, looking at him again.

"Hello," I said to him.

"Shut the door," he said in response, looking away from me and forward again. I felt anything but welcome or comfortable as we pulled out into traffic and drove away. Welcome to Kiev, I thought to myself.

The ride to his home was rather long and awkward. He lived in a rather drab area of Kiev, well outside of the city centre, in a block communal building. My attempts at engaging Riazi in any small talk or dialogue during the drive were completely futile, as he would only respond with a nod and a yes or a no. His abode was a one-bedroom apartment on the fourth floor with no elevators, only stairs. The place seemed like a relic of a bygone area with many historical artifacts, antiquities, and of course, stacks of books and newspapers everywhere. It completely lacked any design, structure, or style.

"Why are all intellectuals so dull?" I thought to myself quietly. Actually, I knew why. Creativity requires imagination, not knowledge.

"You have the couch over there. The bathroom is over there, and there's the kitchen. You can smoke inside," he said, the first real sentences he had made, which felt more like a directive or instruction. I nodded in agreement, not caring where I slept, as I knew I would not be staying here very long. I had just arrived, but already felt uncomfortable and was somewhat regretful of my decision. Perhaps Uncle Ammad was right about this all. It was too late anyhow.

"You're hungry?" he asked me.

"No, I'm fine. I wouldn't mind a drink, however. Do you drink?"

He took a step forward, his eyes fixed on mine. "Are you being smart?"

Caught off guard and confused, I wasn't sure what he meant. "I'm sorry?" I said.

"I'm not some religious fanatic or fundamentalist who thinks that alcohol is a sin. I fought those people. Even killed a couple. Of course, I have alcohol. What are you, stupid?"

I was rather stunned by his demeanour and tone of voice. What was his problem? It was only a damn question.

"I didn't mean to offend you," I said. He continued staring at me with condescending eyes, almost snarling.

"Top shelf above the fridge. And drink the green bottle, not the red one. That one's rare and I doubt you would appreciate it." What a complete asshole? I thought to myself. "I am going to take a nap. Don't make any noise" he said, disappearing behind the door adjacent to the couch.

I had not expected such harsh treatment from him. I was his best friend's son after all, did that not count for anything? Taking a couple of stiff shots to wake me up, I showered next, shaved, and put on a fresh outfit and stepped outside on the tiny balcony for a cigarette with a glass of vodka on the rocks.

I was on my fifth or sixth drink – I needed them to make my present situation tolerable – when I heard a creaking noise behind me and looked back to see that Riazi had emerged out of his lair, not looking at me, but walking straight across the hall to the washroom. Quite a long nap, I thought to myself, looking at my watch and realizing it was past 9 p.m. A few moments later, he emerged onto the balcony, allowing me to really get a good look at him. An imposingly large figure with a heavy aura to him, he wore his years rather well.

"You hungry?" he said very curtly, not blinking once. "Sure," I responded. I was actually famished. He walked out of the balcony and into his room, I presumed, to change. I downed my final drink and got up, feeling slightly dizzy as I did, realizing I had been sitting and drinking for a couple hours. I always found it funny how our generation treats this like a normal activity nowadays, drinking. We seem to imbibe ourselves regularly and plentifully. Judging from my own experience of living back home in the city, it almost become a necessity, the essential social lubricant without which society's gears seem to get stuck. Do we love it or just need it?

After a short drive, we approached a plaza area that had a variety of shops and restaurants within it. The weather was damp with a slight drizzle, but warm. Parking at the end of the lot, we walked towards the opposite end of the plaza and into a restaurant by descending a level of stairs, underground. The place was completely lacking in any design and was painted maroon red, but it was rich in aromas.

We sat down, and a young woman with blonde hair came over and attempted to give us two menus, but she was stopped by Riazi immediately as he proceeded to order various things in Ukranian right away, only stopping at the end to ask me if I ate meat.

"You're not some new age vegetarian fool, right? You eat real food?"

"Yes, I eat real food," I responded, wanting to ask him what his problem was. "I only eat fake food on the weekends," I said back sarcastically, eliciting a glance from him. I was growing irritated by his ways.

Shortly thereafter, two large pints arrived, which he took a sip of without even toasting me. Placing it down on the table heavily, he went into conversation.

"What are you looking for boy?"

"What do you mean?" I responded.

His eyes pierced mine. "I'm an old man, I don't have the time or energy for bullshit or small talk. Why are you here?"

I decided to abandon any further attempts at building a friendship or being polite with him. Some people just aren't worth it.

"After my father died," I began, "his lawyer gave me some folders of his containing private documents. Notebooks, journals, pictures. I've gone through some of them now and there is much in them that I cannot make sense of." He was looking away. "I was hoping you could help me with them since you knew my father as well as anyone."

By now, a different waiter had brought us an appetizer, some pickled vegetables and some form of skewered meat which I really did not care for, but Riazi consumed with gusto as if he hadn't eaten in days. Not lifting his head while doing so, mouth full of food, he finally spoke.

"What do you want to know, boy?"

Leaning forward, I said, "There is a girl and a woman in several pictures that I do not recognize at all and whose identities I cannot figure out. Father also refers to feeling guilty for leaving certain people behind in a couple of passages."

Riazi continued eating, his head still lowered and focused on his plate. I wasn't sure if he was actually listening to me or not which was frustrating.

"Do you know who this young girl and woman are then or not?" I said a moment later.

He stopped eating, took a large sip of his beer, and looked at me. "If you're your father's son, you must have half a brain at least. I'm sure you can figure it out."

What the hell did that mean, and why did he keep calling me "boy"? Just as I was about to ask him what he meant, the main courses arrived.

"Let's eat," were his next words, infuriating me inside as I clenched my hands tight. 10 minutes later, we were done and Riazi lit up a cigarette, and I followed suit.

"Look," I said finally, "I'm not sure how I've upset you, that is not my intention, but you are the only one that can shed light on my father's life for me and these files."

He looked at me, cutting through the smoke dancing between us with his deep, dark eyes and heavy look.

"Your father was a good man, a brilliant writer, a great journalist. He was my only friend. They killed him. They killed him in the worst way, butchering his body and ravaging his soul, but not finishing him, leaving him hanging in misery like a loose strand. What more do you want to know?"

He took a long puff of his cigarette, but his eyes remained fixed on me like a sniper on a target.

"I want to know who this young girl and woman are, Riazi." It was the first time I called him by name. He sat forward, ashed his cigarette in the steel ashtray, blowing the last puff towards me.

"Are you really this simple, boy?" He smiled wryly, chuckling even before sitting back and crossing his hands, leaving me completely confounded. I stared at him for a moment, while he stared at me, neither of us phased by the young girl dropping off the cheque during our standoff. "Let's leave," he said, dropping some bills on the table.

Stepping back outside, the temperature felt cooler than earlier, giving me a slight shiver, or perhaps it was just his energy rubbing off on me. He suggested a light stroll around the corner on a side street which sloped downwards. I followed, of course. It was rather quiet with the odd person here or there. He took out his cigarettes, tapping the pack on his hand twice, pulling one out and lighting it. We finally stopped walking. He was standing directly under the street light, casting him in a dramatic pose. He would make a good villain, I quietly thought to myself.

"Look," I said, "I'm not sure what is going on here, what you and my father were involved in or even if you like or respect me, but…" at which time he interrupted me and said, "Shut up, boy." I was completely caught off guard by his statement.

"Excuse me?" I said back to him in a sharp manner.

"You heard me," he responded as he took another puff of his cigarette. Dropping it on the ground and stepping on it with his black leather shoes. Choking it with a twist, he stared straight at me now, questioningly with furrowed eyes and pressed lips.

"Remember," he began, "you asked for this, and because your father was a man I respected above all others, I will do you this favour because of him."

I felt my heart race a bit and my muscles constrict and tighten. Anxiety overcame me once again, alongside anticipation. Why was he so dramatic? What was he going to tell me anyways? He took a few steps forward and stopped, looking at me straight in the eyes.

"That is your father's other family, his other woman and the daughter he shared with her."

The human mind denies things which it finds overwhelming sometimes. In more extreme cases, it simply shuts off, and the person faints. I don't even think I blinked or breathed as I tried to make sure I heard him right.

"Excuse me?" I said, squinting at him with confusion. "What do you mean other family? I am his family, my mother, my siblings."

He looked at me, but said nothing.

"Hey!" I yelled at him. "What the hell do you mean other family?"

He was a bit stunned, but kept his position. "He had another family. You guys simply haven't known about it. It was his secret that he kept from you."

I gulped, shaking my head and repeating the word "no".

"That is ridiculous. That is fucking ridiculous. You can only have one family!" I shouted again, my tone shrill. He just continued to stare at me, not uttering a word. I wanted to shout at him again, curse him, damn him for saying what he had, but I suddenly felt mute and unable to speak, gesturing with my mouth and tongue in a bizarre manner as if I was having a seizure.

"Damn you, God, why?"

Placing both my hands on my face, the tempo of my heart racing noticeably as my vision became hazy, my legs began to buckle. Unable to speak again, nor breathe, dizzy, I finally dropped to the ground. Riazi, perhaps realizing that I was about to collapse, stepped forward to preempt my fall. He was too late. I fell back, first against a light pole, then sliding around it and teetering like a big tree whose trunk had been cut. I hit the ground with a thick and heavy thud. Some truths are just too heavy to hold up. Some lies cut too deep to withstand.

"Wake up, boy, wake up." I heard, followed by a few hard slaps to my cheeks. For a moment, I thought I was in Turkey again with Uncle Ammad beside me on the couch. Coming to, I quickly realized where I was and who I was looking at. Behind Riazi, I saw a couple who were staring at me with concerned looks on their faces.

"Wake up, boy, you're embarrassing me. This isn't Canada, you can't do these things in public here. Get up."

I was quite groggy, lethargic, and lying down on a sidewalk in Kiev. Could it get any worse? Using all my strength and a hand from Riazi, I managed to sit up and rest my back against a building. I started to regain my composure and stood up slowly, slightly dizzy, but in control of my body again. It was odd for me to faint. Sure, the revelation was shocking, but I'm sure the excessive drinking, poor diet, and lack of sleep were all factors.

"Let's go, boy, we can't stand around here like this, not in a country like Ukraine."

I marshaled my strength and made my way around the block and into his car. We drove off towards his apartment. Enervated, still in shock, I actually wondered several times whether I was dreaming or not. Sadly, I was not, he had spoken the truth to me, and it made sense now.

"You get those bruises from fainting too?" he said to me sarcastically. Confused at first, I quickly realized he was referring to the cuts on my face from the thugs in Turkey. It dawned upon me just then that he had never even asked me about them until now. Was he not curious? Perhaps he simply did not care. I found it fitting that he was my father's best friend. They shared much in common after all it seemed.

Back in Riazi's apartment, I took a seat on the couch that was supposed to be my bed for the night. He brought out two glasses and the bottle of vodka from which I had been drinking earlier. Pouring two drinks, he grabbed one and handed it to me.

"Drink it," he said sternly. I did, in one gulp.

"Another one, please," I said to him as I placed my cup forward again. He obliged, graciously filling my cup halfway.

"This is what happens when you pry into the past, boy. Much rises to the surface that is better left under it, especially with a person like your father." I continued to look forward, a blank stare on my face. "Don't expect me to feel sympathetic towards you for this. Believe me, your life has been pleasant compared to mine and his."

I had to stare at him. Who the hell was this person? How could he be so presumptuous? What did he know about my life? What does anyone really know about anyone else's life?

He knocked his drink back and spoke again. "Your whole generation is spoiled. You won't have to endure what we did when we were your age."

There was much I wanted to say, but I was too tired, I was too emotional. Reason and calm are the first to jump overboard in a ship that is sinking with emotion. Better to bite my tongue, I convinced myself, taking another sip. My thoughts and feelings shifted between shock, pain, and anger. I was angry at my father for his actions, his indiscretions towards me and my family, my mother especially. Just when I had found out that perhaps there was some good somewhere in this man after all, I was quickly reminded of what a depraved, despicable man he truly was. How could he have another family outside of ours, and another child with another woman? How does a man do that and live with himself? He obviously abandoned them also. He must have; they certainly didn't live with us all these years. What kind of scoundrel was he? Did he not hurt my mother enough? At this point, something came across my mind. I sat up in thought. I wondered if my mother knew about this all, especially recalling how she had reacted when I had first brought this all up with her back in Toronto.

"My mother," I said to him, turning to my left to face him and catching him off guard, "does she know?"

He didn't answer at first.

"Well, does she know or not?" I asked again, louder.

"I don't want to discuss this any further," he responded finally. "Let it go. It's history." He seemed exasperated and dismissive.

He got up and paced to the balcony, but I got up and shouted at him, "That's easy for you to say, isn't it!"

He turned around and placed his sharp eyes back on me. "Easy boy. Don't get smart with me, I didn't create this situation for you, remember."

We both went silent, staring at one another, until I finally implored him: "Please, does she know?" I was at my breaking point.

"Yes," he finally responded, "she found out eventually, but only after you had all fled from Iran."

I nodded my head gently. "So she knew all along, all this time," I said in complete disarray, feeling betrayed by her once again. She hadn't told me about what my father had done in the camps, and now this. How could she of all people do this to me? I felt completely overwhelmed by everything that had happened in the last week or so, and now this. Perhaps everyone was right, that nothing good comes from prying into the past. That you can only trust yourself.

"Here, have another one," he said to me as he poured me another drink. I had tears on my face, which he noticed. "She was probably just protecting you all," he said.

"It doesn't matter," I responded. "She had no right to keep this from me and my siblings."

He paced back towards the balcony door and lit another cigarette. "You want one?" he gestured by extending the pack out towards me. I nodded my head.

"Riazi," I said to him, standing up to face him, "Where are they now?"

"Where is who?" he responded.

"This woman and this young girl?" I realized she wouldn't be a child any longer.

He stared at me, then outside as he blew his smoke.

"I don't know," he said in reply. He was lying. I could sense it.

"Please tell me, I need to know."

He stared at me and repeated again, "I really don't know."

What could I do? "Is there anyone else that might know?" I asked him.

"The only other person is your Uncle Manokin, in Iran."

I was confused by this. He was my father's younger brother, and he was not on good terms with him. One was a communist, one was a devout person of faith. They were like acid and water.

"Why does he of all people know?" I asked.

"Your father left them in his trust after you all fled Iran. He really had no choice," Riazi responded. I continued staring at him. "My suggestion, boy," he said, "is to leave this all where it is and stop chasing it. You won't find them, but even if you did, then what? You will be complete strangers."

These words penetrated me deeply. He was right. I had a stepsister somewhere in the world, but I had never met her. I did not know her. I was utterly defeated. I sat down on the couch once more in this apartment in Kiev with my late father's best friend. I had no idea what I would do next. I felt despondent once again. My head hung low, literally.

Riazi had gone into the bedroom and emerged with a light sheet and a pillow. "Get some sleep. Tomorrow's another day," he said.

"Until one day it's, not" I thought, perhaps even hoped.

The next morning, Riazi walked into the room and noticed that I was awake.

"Coffee?" he asked me.

"No, I'm fine," I responded back. I felt no better this morning than I did last night, perhaps even worse. I had barely slept. The weight of what I had found out last night had sunk and settled deep within me.

"What are your plans for today?" he asked me. I merely shrugged in response. "You can stay here and do what you need to. I'm heading out for a few hours." He retreated back into the kitchen, but continued talking to me. "I wouldn't go outside if I were you, however. It isn't safe. They don't like our type here."

Where the hell was I going to go anyways? He eventually left without telling me when he might return, or even saying bye for that matter. His apartment was even more depressing in the daylight. I got up to find my cigarettes and my anxiety pills. Taking a pill out of the bottle, I chucked it in my mouth and swallowed it by knocking back my head, without water.

Coming back down, I caught myself in the mirror. I stared at my face, studying it as if it was someone else's. "Who are you?" I asked myself. I wasn't sure anymore. We all lose our way at one point or another and find ourselves asking this question. It is the most important question of all, one few people can answer comfortably or accurately if you asked them. I certainly could not. At least not anymore. What happens when you no longer recognize yourself? What do you do?

The phone rang several times before someone picked up. It was my younger brother, Nuri. We had kept in touch via social media, but hadn't spoken since I'd left Toronto. It was nice to hear his voice. My brothers were like children to me. In the absence of my father, I had essentially acted like one to them. He didn't know much about what was going on and I wasn't going to burden him with it all.

After a few moments, he finally passed the phone over to my mother, who was quite eager to talk to me naturally. It had almost been a week since we last spoke.

"Moshe, my boy! I miss you. How are you? How is Turkey?"

I had no choice but to be upfront and tell my mother why I was in Turkey, why I was now in Ukraine, and what I had found out. I didn't feel all that bad doing so either as I felt betrayed by her, something I never thought I would feel from my mother. Wasting no time, I spent 15 minutes or so bringing her up to speed on everything. I don't think she quite believed me at first, but eventually realized that I was indeed telling the truth. She began to cry, which complicated everything.

"Mom, please, stop crying. How do you think I feel right now, having come halfway across the world only to find this out?"

"Moshe," she said in response, "I didn't want you to go searching for all of this for precisely this reason."

We spoke a few more sentences, and she kept insisting that I should drop it right now and return home and let it all be. I bit my tongue several times, but I couldn't handle it any longer and finally snapped.

"No, God damn it! This is wrong. I'm sick of you telling me to leave this behind. I'm not a boy anymore, stop treating me like one." She went silent. I kept going as I was worked up. "How could you keep this from me, mother? From all of us, all these years? How?"

I heard her whimper on the other side, unable to say anything. I felt horrible about inducing such a state in her and became upset with myself for it. I was frustrated by the whole situation and finally hung up the phone as she continued on. I stepped onto the balcony to light a cigarette, but the lighter was empty. I threw away both items and slammed my hand against the rail and swore several times. Why was this happening to me? What a nightmare. I felt terrible for hanging up on my mother. That was something completely out of character for me, though then again, so was feeling betrayed by her.

I went back inside and dialed her again. She picked up quickly. Closing my eyes, I took a deep breath and said, "Mom, I'm sorry."

"It's okay," she responded.

"You have to realize this is incredibly hard and painful for me to find out now, after all these years. You had no right to keep it from me, to keep it from all of us."

She didn't say much. What else could I do? She did apologize, several times.

"What's done is done," I said. "You can help me though. You can help set this right a bit."

"What is it, Moshe? What can I do?"

"I need to know where they are, mom, the girl and the woman."

"I don't know my boy, I really don't," she responded.

"You have no idea whatsoever?" I asked next.

"No, I don't, please believe me."

Of course I would, she was my mother. If you couldn't trust and believe your mother, what would you be left with in life?

"Then I need your help with something else."

"Anything," she said. "Anything, my boy."

"Riazi told me that Uncle Manokin is the only other person who knows anything about all of this. That he took care of them or something after we fled Iran. I need to see him. I need to go to Iran. I need you to arrange this for me, please."

The line went silent right after I had said this. "Mother?" I said again.

"Moshe, please don't do this to me and yourself. Don't go to Iran. It isn't a joke, it could be trouble for you after all these years."

Perhaps she had a point. Who knew how the Iranian government would receive me so many years later, especially if they realized who my father was? Such precedents had already been set before. Not allowing this to become an impediment, however, I convinced myself and her that it wasn't an issue.

"It's been 23 years," I said, "and I'm a Canadian citizen now. I'll take my chances."

She did not give up. "I beg you, please, let this go and come home."

Perhaps she was right, I thought to myself. Had I really achieved anything by discovering what I had thus far on this journey? Was it going to help my life moving forward at all? Would this remove my emptiness and bring meaning to my life? It could just as well end up hurting me.

That was a risk I was prepared to take however. I had a stepsister for God's sake, someone with whom I shared a genetic heritage with, albeit a partial one. How could I just go on knowing that she was out there somewhere, living life like me, but that I would never know her? I couldn't, I knew myself too well. You have to know yourself well in life. Self-knowledge is the best protection there is from all the ills of man. "Know thyself" said old Socrates. None was wiser than him.

My mother continued to implore me not to go to Iran. I hated upsetting her, but my mind was set on this. She finally ceased from trying to dissuade me and agreed on my request to call Uncle Manokin. Thanking her, I told her I would call her back within an hour to see what progress she made. In the meanwhile, I would find a flight to Iran. It hadn't sunk in quite yet, but it did just then. Was I actually going back there? The country I was born in. The country my family fled 25 years ago. I needed to complete the circle of my father's life and that of my own. One will always return to where or what they are from, one way or another. I would find this woman and this young child, my stepsister that he so callously brought into this world and then abandoned. Uncle Manokin was my final hope of getting to the bottom of everything once and for all. Nothing about this part of my journey was going to be easy or without risk. It was time for me to go back to my roots, quite literally. I was headed to Tehran.

Chapter 10:
The Truth

The captain had just announced in English and Farsi that we were approaching Tehran International Airport. I had difficulty believing what I just heard. 25 years have passed since my family was fleeing this turbulent country on pickup trucks and horseback across dangerous terrain towards Turkey. Our destiny was forever changed because of that journey. A life can have more than one destiny; free will makes this possible. I had spent the better part of yesterday in Kiev. It was complicated getting a visa to visit this country, but luckily, I was Canadian and not American and the Iranian consulate in Kiev approved my visit on the very same day, albeit with a hefty charge. Mother had reluctantly arranged the meeting with Uncle Manokin. I had asked her to relay to him that I was coming in for a quick and quiet visit to see him and settle various matters regarding my father's estate. Everything had been quickly arranged, including a pickup from the airport.

We were descending into Tehran; it felt quite surreal as my head hugged the window and my eyes hugged the many large mountains surrounding this storied and important city of 12 million. It looked different than I had imagined it would, even from up here. Then again, there is always a difference between imagination and reality. My thoughts were of my father as well. How could they not be? He once played a prominent role in this place and tried to change it, only to have been nearly killed and forced to flee.

The plane shook quite a bit as we neared the ground, giving me a brief scare and I'm sure the other passengers as well. Finally on the ground, I laid my head back and sighed. I wasn't sure if I was relieved or nervous. 25 years, I thought to myself again. Where does time go?

I had been worried about passing airport security, given that I was a first-time visitor after all these years and because of my family name. I knew others that had been held up and questioned in the past, but luck seemed to be on my side today as I passed through with merely a series of questions, all of which I readily answered the female guard, who wore a headscarf and a hollow expression. The airport was incredibly hectic and busy, but relatively modern.

I made my way outside into the exit area where eager family and friends waited for their loved ones. Isn't this particular spot always a happy place? I was looking for my Uncle Manokin whom I had seen about 7 years ago last when he had visited Canada for a summer to potentially pursue immigrating there. I was overwhelmed by the heat and the crowd, keeping my eyes open while walking into this pavilion full of loud people and young children. Iranians are incredibly expressive and animated people. Looking all over, I finally noticed my uncle waiting for me at the very back by an exchange machine, waving his arms with a faint smile. He wasn't too exuberant about seeing me; that wasn't in his character. Acknowledging him with a wave, I walked over, noticing that he had put on quite a bit of weight and grown an even thicker, heavier beard that was completely white. Uncle, like my father, his brother, was also completely bald, but that is just about all that they shared in common. We shook hands and exchanged three kisses, an Iranian custom, and then headed outside to where he was parked.

Stepping out into Tehran, I was hit with thick humidity and extreme brightness from the sun. Reaching into my blazer, I pulled out my sunglasses and put them on and simply stood still for a moment.

Surveying the landscape, a torrent of nostalgia and emotion washed over me. I could hardly believe where I was.

"Let's go," my uncle said, "we can't leave the car parked there for long."

I grabbed my bag, breathed deep and well, and walked towards a small white vehicle of an older vintage. The door creaked as it opened. I threw my bag on the backseat and got in.

"Seatbelt, please," he said to me.

"It's good to see you, uncle," I said. "Thank you for picking me up and for keeping my visit discreet."

He looked over at me askance, making me feel uncomfortable.

"What is it?" I asked him.

"You haven't been here for 25 years and you want to remain undercover? That isn't right." I had been worried about this. "Do you know how many aunts, uncles, cousins, and nieces you have that would love to see you again, to meet you? How do you think they will feel when they find out that you were here later on?" I couldn't even disagree with him, he was right, but he did not quite know what I was here for either and what I had been through recently. "It is morally wrong. God would not approve."

Now I really remembered Uncle Manokin. He was intensely religious and pious, a devout Muslim all his life. He never missed one prayer.

"Uncle, I will explain to you when we get home." He merely looked at me with a blank stare, but said nothing.

Tehran traffic was as hectic as I had ever seen anywhere. There were no lanes in fact, and half of the cars on the road were from the 80s and well past their lifespan, churning out copious amounts of exhaust that left a thick film of smog in the air. We had been driving about 40 minutes when we finally arrived in the lower suburbs of eastern Tehran, hardly an upscale neighbourhood. Pulling into a long, but narrow street, it was lined with Jacaranda trees on either side in front of the cement walls, which were gates to each home, something unique to Tehran. I faintly recalled this. It's incredible the things we remember sometimes, so long after their sense impressions have come and gone.

We parked and got out and walked a few steps to uncle's home. He opened a thick wooden door into a yard that contained a small pear tree, a small, a round blue fishpool with several fish and lilies, and a set of stairs leading downstairs on the left, and a similar, but smaller set on the right that led into house. It was from this area that a woman in a traditional black garb emerged, her face largely covered. It was my uncle's wife whom I had effectively never met, Haleh. I smiled courteously, saying hello and approaching her, unsure as to whether I should hug her or extend my hand. I chose the latter, but much to my surprise, she simply nodded and said welcome to Iran. I couldn't tell if she wore an expression when she said this, only her eyes were visible. It was an awkward moment. I thanked her and nodded with a smile, looking back at my uncle, who stood there just staring at me. He was that much of a zealot that his wife was not allowed to touch other men.

"Let's go inside now," he said. "Prepare dinner for us shortly," he uttered next, not even bothering to use her name, nor look at her. She obeyed immediately, turning around and walking back in.

He showed me my room, a drab little square near the end of the hall that had nothing in it but a bed, a dresser, and a religious scripture on the wall. In fact, the whole place could be described as such, save for a couple beautiful Persian rugs. There were no windows in this room. It seemed more like a prison than a bedroom. I settled in, washed up, and made my way back into the living room area, crossing my uncle's room along the way who I noticed on the floor, prostrated and praying. I walked back to the kitchen and saw my aunt feverishly preparing dinner. It smelled quite aromatic, scents of turmeric and rosewater permeating the air, enticing my senses.

"Can I help with anything?" I gently asked her, startling her as she turned around and seemed nervous, pulling her garb ever tighter to herself.

"No," she said tensely. "Please," she said, pointing to the living room. What could I do but smile and nod.

I was looking at some very old pictures on the mantle of people whom I did not recognize when my uncle grabbed my attention by speaking to me from behind, turning me to face him.

"Let's eat, it's getting late."

We made our way to the table, sitting down to an incredible spread of basmati rice, stewed lamb curry, and various Persian condiments and appetizers.

"Where's Aunt Haleh" I asked my uncle.

"She'll eat later in the kitchen. Eat while it's warm," he said curtly without even looking at me as he proceeded. I couldn't quite believe how much of a mysogonist he was. This wasn't rare behaviour amongst a certain type of religious men in Iran towards women, or in parts of the Middle East at large, sadly. To this day, women remain second class citizens in many parts of the world, a continuing blight on our species. I began to serve a plate for myself and also began to eat. Neither of us said anything while we ate.

Afterwards, we retired to the living room, where his wife brought tea and dates.

"Thank you," I said as she again silently nodded and walked away. Uncle was looking at me with a stare, inquisitive, perhaps suspicious.

"What is it, uncle?" I asked him.

"You still lack faith, like your father."

Unsure how to answer, I merely deferred doing so, drinking my tea instead.

"Do you think you will always be young?" he said. "Do you not fear death, or ending up like your father?"

I couldn't believe he had just said that as I looked at him with a cold stare.

"What does that mean?" I said, wondering how he could be so callous. "I am nothing like my father, and as you know, he is deceased. How about some respect?" I put my tea down on the table.

"You're an intellectual, right, like your father?" my uncle said. What the hell did that even mean? "You all think you are above God's rules and commandments. You all end up the same."

How does one respond to such comments, to such people? With certain people, it is better simply not to argue, as there is no chance for a reasoned discussion. We all come across them and know it, but often persist and do so anyways. Pride is a powerful drive and often will not allow us to admit defeat or resist battle, even when we should or must. I would let him have it and abstain from talking further. After all, I was here for information that only my uncle might have and I did not want to upset him.

"Uncle Manokin, I did not come here for this discussion, with all due respect."

"What did you come here for then," he said, picking up his tea. "Certainly not to see family."

I had to think about it, how to let him know what I had found out and what more I was looking for from him.

"Did you talk about anything with mother, at all?"

He nodded; he really didn't know why I was here. Sitting on the edge of the seat, I put my hands together and spoke.

"Look, uncle," I said, "I need to know certain things about my father, things that I know you know."

He kept staring at me. "What exactly do you want to know that I apparently know about your father?" he said, firmly squaring his eyes on mine.

Feeling uncomfortable, I had no choice but to tell him everything. I told him all that I had come to discover about father and the past on this trip, including, of course, what Riazi had revealed to me about his secret family. Suddenly, at this point, we were interrupted by the sound of glass shattering, which rattled me and drew up my head and eyes in its direction, the kitchen. Uncle had gotten up immediately and lumbered over there. I got up and paced a few steps myself when I heard him shouting a few words, the specifics of which I could not make out. I inferred from the tone and volume that he was clearly reprimanding her. I stood before them, unable to resist peering in. He was hawking over her shouting, and she stood absolutely still, her head down in shame, or fear. What an asshole, I thought. Poor woman, what she must endure. I felt quite uncomfortable.

Then I realized what may have resulted in her dropping the plate. She had likely heard me tell my uncle what I knew. She walked out of the kitchen upon my uncle's command, moving promptly towards the outside door and exiting. My uncle also walked back and past me in the hallway without even looking at me. I followed him back to the living room, and we both took our seats again.

"What happened with Aunt Haleh? Is she alright?"

He simply stared at me once more. "What have you come here for?" he said. "What is it that you think you know?" Was he challenging me?

Instead of answering him, I excused myself briefly and went to my room and brought back the folders and threw them on the table. I laid them out for him to see bare. His unflinching façade broke slightly as he showed interest in the pictures and picked one up to stare at, one of the girl.

"How did you get these?" he asked, continuing to look at the pictures.

"His lawyer gave them to me after he passed away," I said in response. There was a long pause.

He finally placed them down and looked at me again. "What do you want from me?" he said next.

I inhaled deeply and sat back, looking at him. "Uncle," I said, "I've been on a journey that's taken me back to Turkey and the camps, to Ammad and Gelareh, and I am coming from Kiev after visiting Riazi."

He knew Riazi from my father's days in Tehran and I would imagine loathed him because of his views. "You saw Riazi, in Kiev? Why on earth would you have gone there to see that lunatic and heretic?" he said, with a look of confusion on his face.

"I had no choice," I said. "I needed to know who this girl and this woman were."

He shook his head and said, "There is no need or purpose for you to have done this. It isn't your business."

I was shocked and livid at his remark, and I couldn't contain my reaction. "Yes it is!" I yelled, standing up and catching him off guard. I felt indignant.

"Sit down and don't raise your voice in my house," he said curtly, gesturing to the couch with his hand, not taking his eyes off mine. I did, slowly beginning to dislike this simple zealot.

"Look," I said, "after I was given these folders, I could not turn my back on them. I could not make my peace with his passing until I did this. That is why I went to Riazi after Ammad told me that he would be the only other person that might know, and I'm glad I went because now I know."

He did not say anything to me at this point, but instead, glanced at the documents then back at me. "If you did not know for this long, then this is how God wanted it."

He was beginning to test me with his callous and ignorant statements. I wanted to lash out at this man and tell him what an idiot he was, how insensitive he was being. I encouraged myself silently to keep my composure, but he finally crossed the line.

"These things should have been buried with your father, he would have wanted it this way."

Seething, lips quivering as if cold, my right fist came slamming down on the table in front of us like a hot hammer on an anvil.

"Who the hell are you to tell me this!" He was caught off guard by this as his whole body twitched. "I have a right to know what that asshole did. I have a right to know where they are, this family that was kept from me. Don't you see that?"

He stood up as well. "Do not curse my brother, your father! He is deceased. This is a grave sin."

What a damn hypocrite, I thought, considering what he said just earlier and drawing the same response from me. I looked at him, breathing heavily, upset. I couldn't contain myself, I sat down and began to cry.

"I need to know, uncle," I implored, looking up at his face as tears streamed down mine. "I need to know how he could do this to us for so long?"

He had sat back down himself and seemed compassionate towards me now, if in the slightest.

"I need to make my nighttime prayer now," he said a few moments later. "Go outside and sit by the fish pond, get some fresh air. I will be out shortly. It is no longer in my hands now, but God's."

I looked at him, wiping my tears as he got up and walked away. What a simple character this man was, who likely slept well every night because he felt himself pious and virtuous. It didn't matter that he wasn't, all that mattered is that he felt he was. Perception is, after all, reality. Ignorance is indeed bliss. Isn't that what society today believes? My generation certainly does. Then again maybe he was right; what the hell do we know anyways.

I proceeded outside for some fresh air as he had prescribed. I could use it. The air in this house smelled of dogma.

The night air was crisp and surprisingly cool for a summer night. I looked up at the sky, seeing a few stars here and there, then closed my eyes and took in a few deep breaths. Making my way over to the pond, I sat down and looked at the fish. I wished I was one, or a bird; don't we all want to be a bird sometimes? The creaking sound of the door interrupted my thoughts, drawing my head up and left in its direction to see Aunt Haleh come in, not noticing me, head down walking towards the door and inside. Poor woman, I thought. Several moments later, my uncle emerged from the house and walked over and sat down on the chair beside me.

"I am going to tell you everything now because it is not my place to keep it from you any longer, now that you know and insist on finding out more. And because God is judging me." I merely looked at him. "Your mother is the only other person that knows this."

I felt the air thicken around me as I had before on this trip. What would I be told now? I looked at my uncle point blank, waiting for what he had to tell me.

"Your father, as I'm sure you know, was a part of a communist party based out of Kurdistan where he secretly travelled to for work." I knew this and nodded. "He had a mistress up there whom he stayed with regularly from time to time. This is the woman you see in the pictures. When the regime began unearthing your father's activities, realizing where his group was operating out of, they began cracking down on the members, killing some and imprisoning others, so that they could extract information from them or use them as leverage."

I was listening with intent, staring at my uncle without blinking, like a child receiving his first lesson about the universe. "When they imprisoned him, you were barely three; it was a tumultuous period for the family. Everyone got caught up in it all, even her." I presumed he meant his mistress. "They bothered her many times, they raided her house many times looking for information and such, though nothing was ever found, to my knowledge at least. When your father was released in 1987 and you guys fled shortly thereafter, this drew the ire of the regime and to get back at him, they went after her."

I was starting to see the ugly ending this was likely headed towards. "You're with me so far?" I had slowly slipped out, but came back to and simply nodded. "Well, to get back at him, they raped her. They beat her and raped her, repeatedly, forcing many indiscretions upon her." I looked down and away, running my hands across my hair. "Do you want me to continue or not?" my uncle asked me.

I looked up, not at him, but straight: "Yes," I said very directly. "I want to know everything."

"May God forgive me," my uncle said before he proceeded. "She became pregnant because of the ordeal. The poor woman became pregnant with an ill-gotten child." Tears formed in my eyes, but I did not move. I could not, realizing the conclusion that followed from this. "The girl in these pictures, she is not your father's child." I began to cry now, dropping my head at hearing this all. "She never was his child, but he felt responsible for her, for them, for what happened."

I felt as though I had just been buried by an avalanche. I couldn't move, I couldn't even breathe clearly, I was completely overwhelmed by what I had just been told. How many of these revelations could I bare? They had unearthed my foundation, I felt, as though I was standing on empty ground.

"Oh my God." I quietly whispered to myself with my head buried in my hands. My uncle was quiet and simply staring at the pond. Finally raising my head up, face flurried with tears, I spoke to him.

"Uncle," I said to him, softly, whispering almost like a child, "I have to see them. I want to see them. Please." He looked at me with a blank look on his face.

"That can't happen," he said.

"What do you mean it can't happen?" I responded. He looked away and said nothing. "Tell me, God damn it, why can't I see them?"

"They killed her," he responded.

My face froze. "You're lying," I accused him.

"Unfortunately, I'm not," he said.

Puzzled, I continued to stare at him.

"When your father did what he did in Turkey, exposing and embarrassing both governments, they went after her in revenge and killed her, leaving the newborn girl behind. It is a grave sin to kill a child, so she was spared."

"And the young girl?" I asked him, desperate for a ray of light.

"Well," he said, looking at me, "the village they lived in couldn't take care of her and contacted our family, as they had your father's information. I went and brought her back to Tehran, quietly of course, as this was all quite dangerous. Me and Haleh raised her as our own for a couple of years, but it became increasingly risky and burdensome with our own two kids, so we found her a good family to be adopted by, in Turkey."

I felt nauseous and dizzy again, completely and utterly overwhelmed with everything I had just been told. I needed a cigarette. I stood up and lit one and paced away a couple steps.

My uncle continued sitting there, counting his beads and reciting some religious prayer. I wish it was so simple as it seems to be for some. I hated his fake piety. Doesn't it often feel like the world is devoid of providence and purpose? And when we say things like it was meant to be, God works in mysterious ways, do we actually believe these things? Who goes to church anymore, and if they do, what are their reasons? A man like my uncle will make sense of this all by not making sense of it, but by attributing it to the divine plan. I had never felt so little faith in humanity as I did just then. I had never felt more hopeless. Life seemed pointless. I sat back down. I felt numb and slowly, no particular emotion or sensation at all, just numbness.

"How could he do this?" I said out loud. "How could he let this happen?"

My uncle looked at me and said, "This is what happens when you have no faith. If he had not committed adultery with that woman, this wouldn't have happened. Do you see why faith is so important now?" He gave me that stupid glance of his. I was reviled by this man and his inane logic and twisted view of the world and human condition. I was too tired and in shock to say much more to him.

"Anyways, I know he wasn't good to you all, especially your mother, but he never recovered from this. He was always torn by this, by having to leave them behind. He felt guilty about it all his life. He carried it with him to his grave. Don't make the same mistake."

I thought about it more as it slowly dawned upon me how much guilt my father must have worn throughout these years with what had happened. It wasn't all necessarily his fault either. Having a mistress may be morally wrong, but it wasn't illegal. I almost felt some sympathy for him. I imagined if I was in the same position, how helpless and guilty I would feel. It was all too much to deal with. I began to wonder if indeed I should have left this all undisclosed, but it was too late for that. What if the truth does not set you free?

Several minutes passed in which neither of us said anything.

I finally spoke. "I want to see her."

He looked at me, "This was over 20 years ago, I do not know the family well enough anymore to help you with this. Besides, what would come of it, so long after? Do you want to put this upon her, a complete stranger, or your siblings, or your poor mother? Just let it go."

His comment angered me. "Damn it, I have a right to know who she is! Who are you, who is anybody to tell me I do not?" I shouted at him quite loudly.

My uncle stood up and said, "Keep your damn voice down!"

I was pacing, unable to control my nerves, my hands trembling, scratching my head as if looking for a solution that was not available.

"No, no, no, I will not. I must meet her, I must see her, It is my right!"

"Calm down, I have neighbours!" he said. What the hell did I care about them? What do I care about at anything anymore?

"Do you want to see a picture of her?" he finally asked me, seeing that I would not relent. I stopped and looked at him and walked in his direction.

"You have a recent picture? Why?" I asked him.

"They send me pictures of her from time to time, along with updates," he said. "We developed a kinship after our time with her, but she does not know about us at all anymore, only the parents do." I didn't say anything, but was pleased he still had contact with her family. "I will be back," he said, turning around and walking inside. I took a seat and lit another cigarette, feeling completely shell-shocked.

A moment later, my uncle emerged with a folder in his hand. "This is a picture from two years ago," he said as he pulled a colour photo out of the envelope and handed it to me. I looked at it. I felt as though someone had just punctured my very heart with a syringe. I felt completely paralysed, frozen stiff like stone, as if I had countenanced the face of Medusa herself.

"Her name is Kanda," my uncle said to me…

Chapter 11:
The Rain

"Oh my God, please, no!" I kept repeating to myself as I emerged from the most horrendous nightmare. Sitting up, breathing rapidly, my body was soaked in sweat, clammy like a wet towel. I was in that in-between state when one emerges from sleep, but is still unsure whether they have. Don't we all love that moment when it happens? Blissfully lost in between two worlds, for just a little bit.

Looking around the room quickly, a staid, windowless cube, I felt as though I was in a prison. Sometimes I felt the same about my condo. I ran my hands through my face, cast aside the grey sheets and sat on the side of the bed. I closed my eyes and there it was again, Anastasya's face, except it transformed into some ugly, demonic creature that snickered and howled at me like a wild beast. Don't the ones we love torture and terrorize us deep down? Love is like a rose whose stem has thorns. To hold it, stare at its beauty, savour its nectar, one has to bleed first by picking it up. Love is pain.

I quickly opened my eyes and stood up, attempting to eject the image and dream out of my head. Last night reappeared to me like a vision. I began to recall everything that Uncle Manokin revealed to me about the twisted life of my father and its many pieces of which I was only beginning to piece together. She came to my mind, this girl, this woman whom I had come to feel something towards of real meaning. This girl who was the unwanted, ill-conceived outcome of an act of malice many years ago in which my father was intimately intertwined with. This girl whom now held my heart. Kanda.

Sitting in the washroom down the hall, my tears would not abate. I wasn't even sure who I was crying for anyways, him or her? Perhaps I was crying for my father, knowing now what he had to bear all these years and what it must have done to him. I had learned so much about him and his life this past week. I used to joke that he was a tragic figure, but his life was an unabashed tragedy indeed. I always felt that I hated him, but not just now. I pitied him perhaps. I felt sad about it all, but I no longer felt hate towards him.

I was startled by a loud knock on the door just then. "Are you in there?" It was my uncle.

"Yes, I am." A silence ensued during which I hoped he would go away, but he did not.

"Well, when will you be done?" he said. Could he not infer that I wasn't faring well?

"I need a few moments, please," I responded, shaking my head in disbelief. Getting up in front of the sink, I washed my face with some cold water, then patted it dry. Taking a few deep breaths and looking at myself, I was disturbed by what I saw. My eyes were puffy, my skin sagged. Quickly peeling myself away from the mirror, I opened the door and stepped out, shocked to see my uncle still standing there.

"What is wrong with him?" I thought as we exchanged glances.

"Do you want to see some family while you're here at least?" he asked me in a hollow condescending manner as I walked past him. I nodded that I did not as I walked away towards my room. His barren stare and gaze left a hole in me as I did so. Does it ever feel like the whole world is against you, that no one understands you? I felt this way as I shut the door behind me with a thud. I wish I was I was alone and no one else existed.

Looking at my watch, it was barely noon. What was I going to do with myself? I had to leave Iran, but to where? Back home to Toronto? That wasn't an option; there was nothing there for me. I didn't feel like travelling or vacationing. Turkey was an option. Kanda was there after all, but who was she to me really and what would I tell her anyways? How could I look at her the same after what I had found out? Overwhelmed and feeling despondent once again, I lay back down on the bed, hoping to drift off into sleep like a convalescent wearied of struggling against a sickness. Every attempt to subdue my mind and slip off into sleep failed.

After 30 minutes of tossing and turning, I was finally exasperated. I reached for my cigarettes and ran outside. I did not encounter my uncle on the way, shutting the door rather hard. I stepped out into an overcast, but warm day. I looked upon this nook, not having really observed it during daylight yet. Everything looks different at night, more free of imperfections because of the darkness. Is that why we come out at night, because everything seems perfect? I heard life on the other side of the wall from the yard. The whirr of traffic, bicycle bells, birds whistling, people walking. Here was another city before me, and it sounded essentially the same. Is not life similar all over the planet, people doing the same thing, living the same existence with just surface differences? I was tempted to go out and see this place of my childhood, to see Tehran on foot all alone, but I couldn't do it.

Sitting on the steps, I lit a cigarette, coughing with the first inhale. I looked at the cigarette, smoke billowing from it like some chimney. It actually repulsed me, this strange object. I took another puff and chucked it. My breathing became heavy once more. I stood up and walked over to the fishpond and stood above it. I recalled what had transpired here just last night when my uncle revealed the truth to me. I had always viewed my father much the same way that most of us view our parents at large, through our own eyes. How could my eyes have ever seen what he had to endure all these years? Knowing the truth, it was suffocating for me to bear. How well do we really know the people closest to us? How well do we know their stories, their truths, and what makes them who they are?

Just then, I heard the door creak open behind me. Turning around, I saw uncle stepping out. Looking away and back at the pond, I quickly rubbed away the few tears that had made their way onto my face. I could see him from just the side of my left eye. I turned a bit more, and he seemed rather daunting from this angle, wide and thick, heavy beard, deep stare. He came walking towards me as I placed my gaze back on the pond.

"How long are you going to sit and cry for?" he said. I remained staring at him, but was unable to say much. "You came here to find the truth, well, you found it. Now deal with it like a man."

Ultimately, he was right. I had to face the music and accept what I had discovered.

"I'm going out for a bit, I'll be back in a few hours."

I simply nodded as he walked away, opening the door and walking out in to the street.

"What an asshole," I said as he stepped out, watching him secretly all the way. We always watch people when they aren't looking. Loathing my present state and location, I began to feel anxious once more. I still had my anxiety pills with me, which I hadn't taken since yesterday. I quickly made for the refuge of my room where they were. I took two of them to ensure that I passed out. I did not want to be awake. No matter how difficult or tiresome life may become, we always have the refuge and comfort of sleep. Is this not why we look forward to it so much?

My eyes opened ever so slowly as I woke up, feeling quite groggy and lethargic. Reaching for my watch, it was just after 5 p.m. I had been out several hours. I sat up, feeling nauseous, probably because I hadn't eaten anything since last night. I heard a few loud knocks on the door. Who could it be, but my uncle.

"Yes," I responded.

He simply made his way in as if I had welcomed him. Standing there and facing me, an emotional mess, he said nothing at first. He continued staring, however, and eventually made his way over and stood above me.

"What do you want?" he said. I merely looked up on him in disdain, this shortsighted creature I was ashamed to consider family. "Do you want your father to return? Do you wish you didn't know what you do now?"

There was a long pause and a stare-off. "What do you want?" he said as he raised his voice and his arms out in questioning. "Everything is God's will."

I looked at him without any hard feelings. I realized something through him. We are all what we are and what we must be. Often, what we have been conditioned to be. What about free will, then?

"Dinner is ready shortly. Don't be long," he said as he walked out. At least he had the courtesy to close the door behind him.

I recalled something a good friend told me when my father had passed many months ago: "It's a new chapter in your life. Close the last one. Write this one well." He was right. My father was gone and I knew the truth. Nothing was really holding me back as it had in the past. In life death, and in death, life. The circle seemed to be complete. There are indeed no beginnings and endings, but transitions and phases. Am I not my father's son, or my mother's? Can we ever truly escape our past, our upbringing? Even physically, we are remnants of what came before us. All life is a continuum. A calm awareness and sense of understanding washed over me, if even momentarily. It is arbitrary when a chapter ends and another begins.

This happens in books, and it happens in life. Regardless, I felt that perhaps this was the end of one chapter and the beginning of another. I got up and made my way for dinner, out of respect for my Aunt Haleh, who once again, had spent the better part of the day in the kitchen cooking.

Sitting down on the ground to another nice spread, I was hungry, but had no desire to eat. Uncle, however, had no problems doing so. Maybe he was a happier person than most because of his simplicity, I thought, as I looked at him, perhaps with a tinge of envy. He seemed to have what we all desperately seek, peace of mind. I had a few bites myself, but food only tastes as good as you're feeling.

I could hear the faint sound of a light rain now, outside behind me, which drew my attention. I turned around towards the window. I couldn't quite make much through the curtains, thick and dark that they were, but I'm quite sure it was drizzle I heard. I looked back at the spread, as my uncle looked at me, a still look on his face, then quickly back at his food. I resumed eating, but after a few more morsels, I heard it again. I heard a light rumble outside, which confirmed for me that it was indeed raining. This actually delighted me. A few seconds later, a large crack and pop rattled us both and I'm sure all of Tehran, as nature displayed her ferocious and loud beauty. I was energized by this jolt and got up, looking at the window with awe as if it was some portal to another realm. My uncle was caught off guard as he looked up at me, but said nothing, continuing to chew.

I walked closer to the window with tender steps as more thunder erupted. The rain increased in tempo. Energized and made excited by it all, I diverted from the window and finally made my way to the door and pulled it open, stepping outside to the thick whirr of the noise of rainstorm. It sounded like thousands of crickets echoing across a rainforest. We tend to forget that hearing nature is just as powerful as seeing her; it just takes more concentration. The weather picked up intensity, and before me was nothing less than a symphony. Thousands upon thousands of bullets of water pounding on the ground in unison like a choir.

Right then, I saw a massive lightning bolt just outside the wall of the yard above me with a penetrating and loud sound that shook the ground and sent tremors throughout my body. I laughed at this, my expression wide like a drunk at the circus, each strike seemingly making me even more excited as if I was a young child.

Just then, for a few brief seconds, a part in the clouds high above me let in some sunshine, whose light radiated the yard, forcing me to close my eyes and embrace its warmth. It left me shortly thereafter, but it had made its point. I stepped forward and down the steps into the yard, immediately overcome with the pouring rain washing over my body endlessly and with no mercy. I couldn't help but smile, and nothing else. I felt giddy, as if I was being tickled. It was the rain; nature was tickling me. Laughing lightly, I couldn't see too well, as I had to keep my eyes relatively closed to avoid the raindrops. I couldn't stand still either, I simply couldn't. I had to dance. I was moving around, erratically, here, there and in circles. I slowly became completely hysterical, laughing, smiling irrepressibly and savouring the pureness of the moment and experience.

For the first time on this trip, I actually felt good. Of course, it had to do with my father and my past and what I now knew. I was free, finally. I was free of my father and of the mystery of his past and that of my family's. I was free of the demons I had confronted on this trip. I was free of the life that I loathed back in the city. My job, my apartment, all the shallow relationships I had developed. My success and its status and trappings had only made me more miserable. The blindfold had been removed now and I saw that I have options. Most importantly, I was free of love and free to love. When you let go of the past and open yourself up to the future, beautiful things can happen and often do. However heavy and hard the truth was, at least I knew it now. Great truths and realizations are often after all discovered with much work and violent upheavals of the body and soul. Something stirred within me.

This great storm under which I stood, it felt as though it was cleansing me of my past. I stood there still and looking up at the sky, engulfed by waters from above. My heart was beating with happiness, while my face brimmed with a smile as radiant and wide as the sun which lay covered, but was near. Even on an overcast day, the sun is always near, its light just behind the clouds which mask it. I had quietly asked the heavens for a sign. They had responded. Everyday is another chance to turn it all around. To write the next chapter and to close the last one. I knew what I felt right now was momentary, but I also knew I had made it through the storm.

Chapter 12:
Childhood Streets of Tehran

Of all counsels in life, time is the wisest. What Uncle Manokin had revealed to me last night was of real significance to me and shook my foundations. Did I now regret this whole journey and my insistence on finding out the truth? Painful and hard as it had been, I did not regret it. Finding truth and meaning in life is of primary importance; we simply forget about these things because modern life makes them secondary concerns. Kanda was the girl all along in these pictures, I still had a hard time digesting this.

Seated on the first step of uncle's courtyard I received a splendid and beautiful morning and sunrise in Tehran. Even the fish seemed elated, swimming quicker in their little ocean. I could not sleep much the night before. The thundershower had left something with me, a desire to find meaning and peace and move forward finally from the past.

Reaching into my shirt pocket, I grabbed my pack of cigarettes, noticing that it was almost empty. I was growing tired of these crutches. That is, after all, what habits and addictions are, coping mechanisms for life. She was the daughter of my father's mistress, conceived in rape, and now I loved her. Only I would end up in such a scenario, I thought to myself, as I chuckled, though it was hardly a laughing matter. It is incredible how someone with so much light within them could have been conceived in so much darkness. That is how full of possibility and potential human life is and can be.

Blowing a thick plume of smoke from my mouth, shaking my head in disbelief about this all, I really wasn't sure what I would do next. I stood up, stretching my hands to the heavens above me, my feet firmly planted on the ground. I let out a genuine sigh as if that might help. There is a particular heaviness in this place. It reminded me of my father. My mind had been so caught up and enamoured with Kanda since I had met her that I seemed to have forgotten about him as a person until now. Where I felt hate for him before, now I felt only pity. He had a lot to bear all his life, much more than I had ever known. What would I have done in his position? In fact, if it wasn't for his action and sacrifice, I would likely still be living in Iran and probably not doing very much with my life. We owe our parents much; we tend to forget this easily nowadays.

I heard Tehran wake up with me slowly on the other side of the wall. I hadn't been here in more than two decades, but I knew about it well through friends and different channels. It was a country undergoing its own unique journey and struggle at present. Legions of youth seeking change, assembling in dark, quiet corners to fight repression, risking life and limb. My father would have been one; indeed, he once was. We take for granted today our liberties and comforts, our orderly life. Perhaps for the first time in my life, I actually and genuinely felt bad for what my father had to go through in his life. I could no longer hate him now.

A motorcycle zipped past me rather fast, leaving an echoing noise. It was startling; I didn't expect him to accelerate so much on a narrow, residential street. Behind the walls of my uncle's yard, I was shielded from the noise and hectic nature of Tehran, but outside of them, I saw how rugged and hurried things were here. No real memories of my first five years here, I felt myself in a new land, a new place, but somehow it did not feel foreign to me. You can't escape your roots I guess. Though I was a Canadian citizen, I was still also an Iranian. It was a heavy feeling being here, knowing that my father would never step in this place again.

Reaching the end of the street, I found the grocery store Uncle Manokin had given me directions to so that I could purchase cigarettes. On the ground before the entrance sat a poor, disheveled old man with a thick beard and torn clothing asking for handouts. Looking at me, he spoke in Farsi, which I understood and asked me for some change. He reminded me of the homeless man I had seen in the rainstorm back in Toronto, or the one we had encountered with Uncle Ammad in Istanbul. It dawned upon me as I stared at this poor man that people are the same all over the world. The human condition is universal, in its beauty and its ugliness. I guess everyone is looking for change in the end, in their lives or in their cup. Taking out the wad of Liras my uncle had handed to me – Iranian money these days is near worthless given the runaway inflation – I gave him few bills.

"Thank you, brother," was his response. I nodded and smiled. I knew absolutely nothing about this man and his story.

A moment later, I emerged from the store and stood on the very corner of the street which I had been told would lead to Azadi Square, or Liberty Square, the most famous area of Tehran. Standing on the sidewalk, my attention was drawn to a small gathering at the other side of the street. Noticing both police and the widely feared Basij militias, I proceeded to cross the street to get a better look. Closer to the action, it was getting livelier and I found it funny that it wasn't drawing a crowd as it might back home. Looking on from under a tree nearby, I realized what was happening. They were chiding a young girl for not being appropriately covered, or something like that. She was with a friend. That seems ridiculous where I come from, but here, it is an everyday reality.

Just as I was listening in and watching with intent, one of the police officers noticed me. He cast me a suspicious stare and gestured to his other colleague that he would be back shortly and began walking in my direction. My back stiffened quickly and I took a deep breath, turning slightly as if to suggest I was facing elsewhere.

"What are you doing?" he said to me, face to face, this tanned figure with an angry, penetrating gaze.

"Nothing, I was just having a cigarette, wondering which way to go to Azadi Square?" I showed him my cigarette, as if that was going to corroborate my story, feeling like an idiot inside.

He continued to stare at me. "Who are you? What are you doing here?"

My right hand was shaking a bit, which I tried to hide by hugging it against my body.

"Nothing, I was, I'm just…" I said, but was interrupted before I could finish by the high-pitched voice of a young man who appeared from our left, saying the name "Ehsan" repeatedly.

"There you are! Where did you go?" he said to me, standing in front of me, this complete stranger. The cop looked at him with the same look, and pointing at me, said "Do you know him?"

The young man looked at the officer and said, "Yes, of course, he's my cousin Ehsan from Germany. He's visiting." He didn't look convinced and stared back at me. I did my best not to look shocked by all this, but I was.

"Officer, it's his first time here. He doesn't understand how things work. Please forgive me; it was my fault, I told him to wait while I went to purchase cigarettes" he said, brandishing the same pack of smokes that I had.

The cop stared at him again and simply said, "Look, this isn't Europe. Keep an eye on your cousin here and make sure he keeps his eyes away from where it doesn't belong. Understand?" He stiffly pointed at him with his baton.

"Of course, sir. I won't let him out of my sight again."

He finally turned around and left us, and I breathed a sigh of relief. Grabbed hard now on the shoulder by this young man who had saved me from certain trouble, he looked at me with stunned eyes. "You're crazy boy. Let's walk," he said as he literally tugged me around and pulled me into motion.

After walking 30 metres or so, I attempted to turn around to see what had happened, but was immediately stopped by this young man again, who yelled at me with a look of astonishment on his face, his eyebrows raised in disbelief.

"Are you stupid or something? Look straight ahead and walk!" I owed him that.

We finally arrived at a little patio up the street where he instructed me in to sit down and quickly ordered something from the server in Farsi, almost as if he knew her. This all felt strange. I was sitting in a café on a street in Tehran on this warm, muggy, sunny day, face to face with a complete stranger. The places we find ourselves in life sometimes.

"Thank you for that," I said to him smiling, trying to convey my gratitude.

"I hope they choke and die, those sons of bitches," the young man responded, looking past me and back in their direction with a face that conveyed nothing but disdain. I wasn't sure how to respond, so I sat quietly.

He looked back at me, inquisitively. "So," he said, "what are you doing here? And why are you here in Iran if you don't know much about it?"

I was confused. "Excuse me?"

"Well, you can't know much about this place if you are standing like a spectator while those scumbags are hassling two young women over nothing."

I think I understood. "You're right, I just wasn't thinking. This is the first time I have been back here in 25 years."

He rolled his eyes at this. "25 years? Wow. Why the hell come back after so long?"

Not sure what to tell him, I simply said that "it was complicated." At this point, we were interrupted by a young, shy woman who brought us two teas and some sugar cubes and biscuits, avoiding making eye contact as she placed them on the table. "Go and clean up the corner table before you go back in, and don't leave any stains this time, okay!" I guess this was his place.

"This is my café. I have a degree in engineering, but this is what I have to do for a living. Bullshit," he said, looking away and shaking his head, clearly frustrated as he placed two sugar cubes in his tea and stirred it. I followed suit. An awkward moment ensued where we both said nothing, but stared at one another. I finally decided to say something, but before I could talk he motioned for me to keep quiet as his head veered right and he muttered some expletives and spat at the ground. I realized that the patrol car had driven by with the two young girls in it and he was swearing at them.

"Was that the girls?" I asked him.

"What, you're blind?" What an irritable young man, I thought to myself, sipping my tea. "They are ruining our country, these ingrates. They are sending us back to the middle ages," he said as he shook his head and sipped his tea. We talked for a bit about things, about life here in Iran, the difficulties faced by its young. Listening to him, I realized I had many blessings in my life as so many of us do, but seldom appreciate. He asked me many questions about western life with zeal, almost as if it was some magical place, some fantastical dream. Of course it isn't. Life is relative and difficult everywhere. Each place has its own unique brand of challenges.

Just then a small blue bird landed on our table. It was a beautiful little bird and I gazed upon it with delight. My delight was smothered quickly, however, as the young man shoved the bird away rather forcefully with his hand as it neared the biscuits. I looked at him, wondering why he was so angry.

"Everyone in Iran is struggling for a bite, even the birds," he said as he finished his tea and lit a cigarette. "So," he said, sitting back, legs crossed and looking brazen like a young Marlon Brando, "what's your name and where are you from?"

Waiting a moment, I finally answered him. "Moshe, from Toronto, Canada."

"Moshe?" he responded, sounding surprised. "Interesting name for an Iranian."

I shrugged. "And you?"

He leaned forward, extending his hand. "I'm Behzad. So what do you do?"

I wasn't sure anymore, but I told him what I used to do. "I'm a banker back home in my city."

He seemed impressed by this as he nodded his head and said, "A Canadian banker, very nice." He stared at me for a moment and I said nothing. "You are very lucky, you know that," he said. That was a subjective statement, but I suppose in ways, I am compared to him and many others around the world. "You make good money, yes?"

I nodded again, not wanting to boast. "Yes, okay money."

"Bullshit," he said to me, laughing wildly, "you make a lot of money I bet. Young guy like you, in Canada, lots of money," he added, shaking his head, almost as if he was saddened by it. "I studied for six years in Tehran University, night and day, engineering, to only to manage this shitty little café" as he gestured around the patio to me as if displaying it. I felt for him; I would not want to be in such a position either.

"It's tough in Iran for the young, I know. I read the reports," I said in response.

He laughed again, looking at me. "You read, do you? You should take a walk by Sanjavi Park if you can sometime. Tell me if the reports are true."

Confused, I wasn't sure what or where that was. "Sorry, I didn't mean to pretend to know how your life is here, I was just trying to make conversation."

"It's alright," he said, waving the conversation away. "Do you know Iran has one of the highest populations of heroin addicts in the world?" I didn't know that. "Yes, in the world, and that's just the beginning of it. You can find just about any drug in Tehran, and cheap. Just go to one of these local parks. They are littered with dealers, addicts, the lost and the destitute, just about anyone from any walk of life in Iran who has been beaten down by this system, which leaves one reliant on prayer alone and not much else for survival."

He was clearly very upset about all this, and rightfully so. I knew what he was talking about. The government lets drugs flow freely into the country from neighbouring Afghanistan, in which Iran exerts a lot of control over, at rock bottom prices, making them cheap and accessible for the population. If people have no jobs, no future, no hope, they can at least have drugs, and of course, this keeps them sedated and hardly able to rebel and fight back. From a strategic perspective, it's a brilliant strategy for the regime. A sordid state of affairs, but such is the allure of power and those with it will do anything to retain it, even destroy a whole country, its people, its future if they must. This is what my father fought for after all, for which he paid dearly.

My thoughts returned to this young man, who was staring blankly at the ground. I asked him if he had ever thought about leaving.

"Huh, of course, but where and with what money? You can't exactly just walk out of Iran." I nodded again, feeling stupid for what I had just asked. "You should be grateful to your father for getting you out when he did." He drew my attention quickly. "It was in the 80's, right?"

I nodded, looking down. "What does he do now?" he asked me next. Caught off guard and shaken by the question, I deferred and asked him a question instead.

"So, listen, what was happening with those girls earlier?"

He looked at me for a moment, then responded. "I'm not sure. They are either selling themselves or perhaps just being picked on for no reason."

"What do you mean, selling themselves," I asked.

"What are you simple? They sell themselves for money, prostitution."

"There must be a serious offence for that in Iran though. Aren't they afraid?"

He looked at me and laughed. "You should stay here for a while, see what poverty and a lack of hope might drive you to do to survive."

I sat back, the weight of his words sinking into me. A heavy thought came upon me just then. I could easily be this guy, and those girls back there could have been one of my sisters. I shuddered at the thought.

"You okay?" the young man asked me.

"Yes, I'm fine. Sorry, just slipped away for a moment."

"Don't worry about it anyways," he said to me. "Tomorrow you will be back in Toronto, and all this will be a dream for you."

He said this with a resignation on his face that pierced me. He looked down on the ground again, the picture of dejection. I kept staring at him, this young guy with thick black hair, scruff, a symmetrical face with thick set heavy eyes and a slender physique slouched on his chair. I genuinely felt for him. Is there anything worse than living a life you do not want nor enjoy, with little prospect for change or betterment, no hope? Even with my life and my problems, I still had it good, as many of us do, but simply never stand still enough to realize. Even if I did not like my present life, at least I lived somewhere where I had the freedom and opportunity to attempt to change it for the better, which itself is a privilege, but in an ideal world, would be a right.

"Behzad," I said, "what is the future of Iran, in your opinion?"

He said nothing for a moment. "Well," he said finally with a serious gaze, "they say that the future belongs to the young." He paused again. "Iran's young are growing older and more weary, and if something doesn't give soon, the future looks dreary."

I continued staring at him as he seemed deep in thought, quiet and reposed, like a young intellectual, perhaps what my father might have looked like in his early days, cigarette and all in hand.

"We don't have much time" he said, shaking his head. We sat there, both of us quietly, almost as if we were longtime friends. He was right, everyday not spent living your dream and passion, or at least pursuing it, is one less day you have to do so. Time is always ticking away after all by natural law.

"Behzad," I said abruptly, "I have to get going." I caught him off guard.

"Something I said?"

"No, not at all, I just want to see Azadi Square, that's all."

"Okay," he responded. I felt bad now; this young man had saved me from certain trouble earlier after all. "Perhaps I can come back later and we can have dinner. I am not far."

He smiled. "Yes, of course. You will be my guest," he said with enthusiasm. I smiled and thanked him.

"How can I get to Azadi Square anyhow? Can I walk?" I asked.

"You could, it's just straight up this street, but it's a few kilometers. A cab ride won't cost much. Want me to hail one down for you?" he offered. "No, no," I responded, "I will be fine. I'll drop in later this evening then."

"Sure thing," he said with a smile. Reaching into my pocket to take out some cash, he motioned for me to stop. "Please don't insult me, you are a guest."

"Thank you," I said, extending my hand.

We shook hands and I walked away. The encounter left me feeling grateful for my lot. I realized it is indeed true, that someone always has it worse than you, often many. My generation needed to learn to be more grateful for what it had. I began walking again.

Traffic in Tehran made Istanbul look like a breeze, even Toronto. I had been walking for a good 35-40 minutes when I finally arrived at the main intersection, where ahead in front of me, I could see Azadi Square. A powerful feeling of nostalgia and awe came over me and I stood still. This beautiful oval thoroughfare of Tehran was its most memorable real estate. It contained a large, iconic, Persian designed structure at its centre that resembled a hollow pyramid with four twisted legs hoisting up a square top. It was built as a commemoration to 2,500 years of the Persian Empire by the Shah in 1971. Everywhere around me were cars, screeching in and out of traffic, honking endlessly, while many people walked around the sidewalks and the small grassy fields surrounding the centre. I recalled walking here with my parents many, many years ago, when I was barely five. It produced in me a distinct melancholy and nostalgia. Taking a deep breath, I proceeded to cross the street by using the pedestrian cross. It was incredibly hot, and the sun was directly above me, beaming down radiantly and selflessly as it has for eons on this land whose people originally worshipped fire.

On the other side, I walked to the centre of this square, standing directly before this beautiful structure. It must be 20 stories tall, at least, I thought. It evoked powerful feelings as all such structures do. They make us aware of just how small we are. I looked upon this, realizing my father likely had done the exact same thing many times. In fact, I was looking at it through his eyes. Parents, are after all literally a part of us and we a part of them. My father had always wanted to return to Iran and see his homeland once more, but he never got the chance to. I began to tear up thinking about this and him. I can honestly say that perhaps for the first time in my life, I felt as though I no longer loathed my father, but in fact, felt something other for him. Perhaps I felt love? Burdened by the weight of my thoughts I decided to sit down and calm myself. Locating an empty bench, I walked over to it and took a seat, facing the monument directly, with the sun shining just behind it, casting a bright and thick aura around it all.

A thousand thoughts, memories, and feelings rushed over me just then and I was helpless to fight them. Perhaps I just didn't want to anymore. We can only run from ourselves and our hearts and minds for so long before they catch up with us and request our attention and reckoning. Never in a million years did I expect to discover what I had on this journey, nor to be sitting here at this very moment. You really never know where life will take you tomorrow. Keep an open mind and don't fear change. I never knew just how lucky I was until now, nor did I know how much my father endured to make my luck possible. And not only me, but many others whose lives he had affected with his actions. One life really can touch a thousand. Each layer of the story I had uncovered sat upon me like a new layer of snow, leaving me feeling thicker and heavier. Had I found my peace with him; was I free of the yolk that was his suffering, and my guilt and anguish for so many years? Tears came forth from my eyes once again, tears that contained in them a lifetime of questions and mysteries which I had always sought, but could never find. This was all nothing less than a revolution of my mind. If the truth was a fallen chestnut waiting to be picked up, I had picked it up and cracked its core to receive its kernel of knowledge: Although it is easy to judge others for their actions, we must do our best to refrain from this until we know the catalyst behind them. There is always more beneath the surface than what appears on top, like an iceberg whose depth below the water is often much deeper than its peak above the waves.

At this precise moment, a seismic shift occurred within me: I believe I forgave my father, and for the first time in my life, felt love towards him.

I was finally interrupted by a tap to my shoulder and an old man's voice.

"Son," I heard as I looked up at an old man who was clearly walking by and noticed me in tears. "Are you alright?"

I quickly tried to regain my composure and rubbed the tears off my face. "Yes," I said to him. Looking upon him, he wore a brown suit and many years. More so, I was phased and frozen by just much he resembled my father.

"Are you okay?" he said to me again.

I blinked several times and snapped out of it. "Yes, sir, I'm fine. Thank you."

He didn't seem convinced. "You sure?" he asked again.

I wanted to just continue staring at him, but I forced my eyes off him, it was too eerie. "Yes, I'll be fine."

He smiled gently and began walking away, carrying my eyes with him as far as they could go. In my culture, they say that when you see someone who resembles a deceased person, it is their soul finding a way to see you. He had disappeared from my sight and into the crowd of people. Maybe I should have spoken to him longer?

Just then, my attention was drawn away and up by a sound that echoed familiarity to me. There it was again, above to my left, a flock of birds flapping their wings and thrusting ahead. I had already witnessed this twice on this journey. They say things come in threes. My eyes were glued once again to these pioneers of the sky, these aeronauts of the spirit, these beautiful creatures of the infinite. I could no longer ignore them and their songs; three times means something. Wasn't there something about the sound of birds after all? Something grounded in science and observation? I thought hard as I stared at them now.

"Yes," I finally exclaimed with joy. "That's it!" I recalled reading somewhere that when scientists had recorded the sound of earth from space, it was eerily similar to the sound of birds. In other words, birds spoke the same language as the earth, and thereby, the universe. Actually, it was the ancient Greeks that had first observed this, I remembered. Yes, Pythagoras, in particular, what he called "the music of the spheres". These birds that had guided me on this journey, was it the universe speaking to me through them? Could it be that the world worked in such ways, that there was some universal language or consciousness that spoke to all living creatures? Yes, of course, there must be; too many things happen that cannot be explained any other way. I suppose I hadn't realized this until now because my antenna wasn't up. It's hard to catch fish without throwing a net into water first. It is no different with us. Our closed minds are drowned in our noisy lives and environments, and we completely miss the symphony of everyday life before us everywhere. Never again, I promised myself just then. We too are creatures of the infinite, just like these wayfaring musicians of the skies.

I stared at them until they were no more, slipping away from my field of sight. Saddened by their disappearance, I wanted to follow them yet again, for they had been kind guides to me hitherto, but I wasn't sure where to. Where are they headed, I wondered? I pulled up my phone and its compass app to find out their direction. It was southwest, just as I had suspected. Realizing what lay in that direction, I concluded that this was another sign. It was unusual for me to make such romantic conclusions, but the truth is that I had been a cynic and skeptic all my life, and what had it got me? After everything that had happened recently, perhaps I needed to try a different approach. Perhaps it was time to have faith in the universe and the signs it presents us with everywhere and all the time if we would only pay attention.

Then and there, having finally made peace with my father, I agreed to leave my past behind once and for all and move forward. I decided I would return to Turkey, and to Kanda.

Chapter 13:
All is Not Lost

Back on Turkish soil, everything about life felt different. The irony of it all wasn't lost on me. I had once again travelled to Turkey from Iran, except this time it wasn't on buses and pickup trucks, nor through backwoods and unpaved terrains wrought with danger. This time, I simply flew over in an airplane. It was still difficult to imagine that 25 years had elapsed between then and now. Stepping outside of the airport and into another sunny, warm Istanbul day, I reached for my cigarettes. I looked at them, almost as if I had never seen them before and simply put them back in my pocket. Eventually, we all have to get our act together and make better decisions. There is no better time to do this than right now, I thought.

Putting my sunglasses on while slipping both my hands in my jean pockets, I stood still and closed my eyes, basking in the sun. Young, healthy, educated, family and friends, opportunities before me, the past behind me, I had it all. What more could a man want from life? For the first time in a long time, I felt grateful and blessed. All was not lost. My moment was rudely interrupted by a cab driver and his horn just then. He asked me whether I needed a cab. Startled, I was upset that my thoughts were disturbed, but I simply nodded, picked up my bags, and made my way towards the vehicle. Providing him with my aunt and uncle's address, I sat back and rolled down my window and looked out at the clear sky, the breeze on my face. Once again, I was on the move, but hopefully this place would be my home for the next little while.

It was just past 4 p.m. as we pulled into the driveway. Uncle Ammad and Aunt Gelareh would not be home until at least 6 p.m. They had left the keys for me under the doormat. I paid the driver and stepped out of the taxi, then walked up to the front door and pulled back the rug to find the key. Stepping inside, the house was quiet and still.

"Hello?" I shouted to make sure I was alone. No response. Making my way downstairs, I threw my things by the couch and had a quick shower to freshen up. The family would be expecting me for dinner when they arrived, so I thought it was a good time to call my mother. She had tried to contact me in Iran, but I was in no mood to discuss my trip with her at the time. I felt like a new man, in some respects. The anxiety and panic attacks, the difficulty breathing, the body tremors, the shaking hands, all of it had noticeably abated over the last day or two. I guess we grow weary even of our weaknesses eventually, or simply succumb to them. What was responsible for this change in me, love or death? Was it making peace with my father at last, or something even simpler, falling in love with her? I suppose it was both. The last few weeks had been the birth pangs of my latest incarnation; we should have several after all in life. All such periods of overcoming that each soul will go through in life are as such, wrought with difficulty and displeasure.

I made my way upstairs and outside into the backyard, stopping to grab a beer from the kitchen on the way. Pulling open the balcony doors, I stepped onto a deck that was luminous with sunlight. Standing at the edge of the patio, I closed my eyes facing the sun once more. Certain thoughts would not escape me still. Would I tell my siblings everything? I had to; I would be a hypocrite if I did not. I wondered how they would react to it. None of them much cared for my father, and frankly neither did I. Then again, I knew very little about him I had come to realize. My perception of him had changed, and I hoped it would for them as well once I told them what I had discovered. My mother, however, was a different story. She knew all that I knew and had kept it from me all these years. I was upset with her at first, but it had dissipated by now. I know in my heart she did what she felt was best for me as any mother would do. After all, she gave life to me. In fact, she gave her life for me, for all my siblings. I owed her eternity, she owed me nothing.

I called her. Several rings later, she picked up the phone.

"Hello?"

"Hi, mom," I responded, a smile dawning upon my face at hearing her voice.

"Moshe, honey, is that you?!"

"Yes, mom, it's me. How are you?"

"Oh, Moshe," she said, her voice filled with the delight, "How are you my boy?!"

"I'm good, I'm good," I responded, happy to hear her once more. "I just arrived back in Turkey at aunt and uncle's."

"I'm happy you made it back safely, I've been praying for you every day." Yes, of course she was.

"Thank you mom, you don't have to tell me, I know you always pray for me."

There was a slight pause. "Mom?" I said, wondering if the line had cut.

"Yes, Moshe. I'm here."

"Are you alright?" I could sense her tone drop a bit.

"I talked to Uncle Manokin. I know you know, Moshe," she said. I wasn't sure of what to say next. "I'm not sure what to tell you," she said in a faint and sad voice, "but I hope it gives you a more balanced picture of things and I hope you don't hold it against me. I had no choice. I had to protect you all."

"I already know that mom," I responded. "I understand why you kept it from me, from all of us. Honestly, I just want to put it all behind us and move forward with life."

I could hear her cry. "Mom, what's wrong?"

"Nothing, nothing at all. I'm happy to hear you finally say that, that's all."

We spoke for several more minutes together, but I did not tell her about my immediate plans, nor about Kanda. Just that I was staying put for a little while in Turkey.

"I have to get going now, uncle and aunt will be home soon for dinner. I'll call you again in a few days." I kissed her across the speaker and told her that I loved her. She told me the same. It was just after 5:30 p.m. The sun was setting and they would be home soon.

The hysterics were endless. Bending over my chair to pick up a brussel sprout from beside my seat at the dinner table, I was hardly able to keep myself composed from the laughter convulsing through me because of Aunt Gelareh's antics. It was late evening, a late dinner by many standards. The family had gotten home shortly after I got off the phone with mother, all three of them, quite happy to see me, including Nav, whom I could finally spend some quality time with, cousin to cousin.

"So," my aunt said, "who could do that from across the table with a carrot?"

"Well," I said, "I could either just throw the carrot instead, or even eat it."

Uncle stepped in, defusing the situation before the carpet became a mess. "Alright, alright, let's just all settle down now and eat the food and not play with it."

"Oh, Ammad," my aunt said, hilariously dismissive with her hands. "You need more wine!" We must have polished at least four bottles already with this dinner. I couldn't recall the last time I had sat down for a meal with people I loved and simply ate and drank merrily, content with life.

"I have to say, Aunt Gelareh," I said, reaching for the bottle of red wine, "Your cooking gets better and better."

"I'm glad you are enjoying it, but you are barely eating. Please, eat some more."

I couldn't possibly. My appetite had shrunk significantly the last few weeks. I was about to stand up and clean when Uncle Ammad stepped in and directed Nav to do so, who at first refused, but then obliged as my uncle threw him a heavy glance.

"We're going to step outside for a cigar," he said, looking at me. I gave my aunt a hearty kiss for the fantastic meal.

"I'll leave the leftovers in the fridge for you," she said as we walked away.

"We'll be outside honey," my uncle said to my aunt as we stepped out back.

It was a clear night, quiet, save for the sound of crickets, the Bachs and Beethovens of nighttime as I called them. "Monte Cristos, only the best," my uncle said as he pulled out two robustos for us, clipping their ends and lighting his up before passing mine over and helping me do the same. I hadn't had a cigar in months. I could see the thick white smoke drift away into the night and above in front of me as I exhaled, drawing my tired eyes up to notice a half lit moon to my right, shining as it does without request.

"Well," my uncle said, "what happened, what did you find out?"

I had mentioned to uncle that I had gone to Tehran after Kiev over email. I stood still, thinking of what to say, whether I should say anything at all.

"Uncle," I said, "do you ever feel like wanting to leave something behind and not looking back?"

"Yes, of course," he said, "doesn't everyone?"

"That's what I would like to do now," I said to him directly. "Leave it all behind me and not look back, not even discuss it."

Uncle had a confused look on his face. He puffed on his cigar, looking away in contemplation.

"You are a big boy," he finally responded. "A smart one, with much experience for your age, so I am not here to preach. If that is what you want, then I will respect it." I felt somewhat relieved he didn't press on. "Just tell me one thing," he said. "You're not my son are you?" He broke into a thick smile and a loud laugh seconds after and had caught me off guard as I was utterly confused before I realized it was a joke. People are incorrigible. We are what we are, now and always.

Waking up, I reached over to my left to look at my watch, an old, gold Omega which belonged to an old friend, Frank, who had passed many years ago. It was only 7 a.m. I wasn't even sure if anyone was up yet. I got up and made my way to the bathroom to shower and change, figuring I would get an early start to the day. I stepped out, wrapped my towel around my waist, and applied some moisturizer to my face, which I patted dry with a face towel. I caught a glance of myself in the mirror. Already I seemed like a different person. More calm, more composed, even happier. My eyes had their old sparkle back. Not only did I feel lighter because of what I now knew, I also felt something altogether more powerful within me, which made my heart flutter. I couldn't wait to see her again today. I picked out some fresh clothes from my bag, some grey trousers and a blue polo and put them on, grabbing my wallet and watch as I left the basement. Upstairs in the kitchen, I was surprised to see my uncle, who had beaten me to the chase.

"What," he said, "you think an old man can't beat you out of bed?"

I chuckled. "Morning, uncle."

"Morning indeed. You're up early," he said.

"So are you," I responded.

"So," he said, "you come back to Turkey a changed man and get up early to go to the camps. I don't get you?"

"Uncle, I told you last night where I would be going today and I asked you not to interfere, remember?"

He simply nodded his head. "I'm actually headed that way today. Simply thought I could drive you." I nodded in acceptance. We finished our coffees and made our way out shortly thereafter.

Pulling up in front of the camps once again, my uncle pulled over to the curb opposite the street he did last time and put the car into park, leaving the engine running. Looking over at me, he asked, "You sure this is what you want to do?" with a serious look on his face. "You sure this is what you want to come back to?"

I looked over at him and said, "Yes, uncle, there is no other place I wish to be than here today."

Noticing just how solemn I was, he accepted this. "I wish you luck then, young man," he said to me, gesturing to the door. I smiled at him faintly, opened it, and stepped out. Peering down and in, I simply told him that I would make my way home later. He nodded and then drove off, leaving me here, facing this place once again all on my own. This time, it did not intimidate me like it did before, and neither was I afraid of it and what it represented any longer. It had been defanged for me, this great beast of my past. It no longer contained gargoyles at its gates.

I had to sign and provide an ID to get in. I did so and passed through the gates one more time. At the top of the steps leading into the main building, I stood still and turned around and surveyed my landscape. I took a deep breath. I smiled at the sky and the horizon before me, and the sun that had been my friend on this wayfaring journey. The world is after all a friend, never an enemy. I finally turned around and walked up the stairs and inside into the building. Walking past the first set of elevators, I made my way down the corridor towards the office where I hoped I would see her once again.

Turning around the corner and approaching the office, I noticed the door was locked, which I found somewhat odd, as it was just past 9 a.m. and the last few times I had come here it was open with several people inside by this time. Looking to both ends of the hallway curiously, there was no one in sight. I knocked on the door. Nothing. I knocked again, but once more, no response. Just as I was about to knock it for the third time, a strong voice from behind me startled me.

"You're back again?"

Turning around, I faced the officer whom I had encountered here on my first visit. I wasn't sure if I was happy or worried to be seeing him.

"Hello, sir." I said.

"Who are you looking for, young man?" he said as he took several steps forward and towards me with his trademark suspicious look.

"I'm actually hoping I could see Kanda again."

"Kanda," he repeated with a curious frown. "Why?"

What would I tell him, that I had grown a deep affection towards her? "Well, sir," I said, "I'd like to volunteer here again perhaps."

Continuing to stare at me, he didn't say much. "Normally, I wouldn't put up with even a hint of bullshit, just so you know."

"Yes," I responded. "I understand. I have only the best of intentions."

He retrieved his phone and called someone, his eyes remaining firmly fixed on mine. I was a bit nervous, not sure who he was calling or what for. He spoke in Turkish, so I didn't understand what he was saying.

"Okay," he said to me as he hung up and placed the phone back in his back pocket. "Come with me." What choice did I have? I nodded and followed him as he walked past me down the hall, not saying a word, until we got through another area and turned right. We were heading towards an exit that led out on the grounds. The ground was damp, just like before. The blue sky balanced the dreariness of this place which I had seen last week. I stood still as he paced forward a few steps, then raised his arm and waved to what I noticed was a small vehicle approaching us. I didn't know what to make of it all, but just hoped for the best. The vehicle finally neared and I realized it was the same one I had rode with Kanda a week ago here.

He finally turned around to look at me. "He will take you to her."

I looked at him as he walked back towards the door. "Thank you," I said, grateful for the kindness this man had shown me since I met him. He looked at me, and finally nodded gently, walking in past the door. I turned around and saw the driver standing there, gesturing for me to board as if the buggy was some chariot. I obliged, of course, and we began to drive off down the narrow roadway towards the building we visited last time.

Looking around at this compound, I realized that I was no longer its prisoner, but rather a willful visitor. Approaching the building, we continued driving past it and around it to my surprise. We were driving down an otherwise open field now, which I didn't have a chance to see last time. I felt as though something about this new area seemed faintly familiar. The general outline of the buildings and the land, and the way they were positioned made me feel as if I had been here before. I began surveying the area at large, trying to get a better picture of it.

It finally dawned up on me. I knew where we were and where we were heading: towards the old, decrepit building where I was raped. For the first time in a few days, I actually felt a pang of anxiety wash over me as I began breathing slightly less easy. I paced around trying to see where the building might be, but it was nowhere in sight, at least as I recalled from my knowledge of the layout and where I thought it should be. It should have been directly ahead in front of me on the right, but all I saw in that direction was a large park area with some grass and what seemed like a playground.

I couldn't quite make sense of it until we got closer, and it began to dawn upon me that this was precisely where it should have been, utterly confounding me. Looking around, it finally hit me. It was here, but it had since been razed. It was, after all, a rundown building, and that was 25 years ago, so naturally they had demolished it by now. My anxiety began to fade, I was somewhat relaxed again. In fact, it may have all been cathartic for me. It was now a large playground and sports field. Immediately in front of me were 40-50 young children playing amongst the park toys.

"Okay," I heard from the driver as I looked back at him and noticed that he was about to drive off again.

"Kanda?" I asked him. He pointed his hand directly at the park area, to which I returned my gaze.

"Goodbye," the driver said to me as he pulled off. I didn't turn this time, barely lifting my hand to gesture my response. I began to slowly move forward, looking around for her. As I reached the edge of the area where the sand began, I noticed a young boy sitting down, gently playing with a small, yellow truck. I recognized him. It was Shuaib, the boy I had seen several days ago inside the compound who had run away from me. Smiling at him affectionately, he looked back at me. Did he recognize me, I wondered? At least he didn't run this time. I knelt down beside him, and with a smile, I said, "Hello, Shuaib." He looked at me, but didn't say anything.

"What have you got there?" I said, pointing to his toy. He picked up the truck and held it for me. I guess it's not just adults that like showing off their toys to others.

"Very nice," I said to him, realizing that he did not understand English. "Shuaib, do you know where Kanda is?" He just stared at me, then back at his truck.

"Kanda," I said again, demonstrating with my hands the outline of long hair and wide smiling face. He stared at me again at first, then finally looked to his right, pointing directly at an area where a lot of kids were. I looked in this direction, squinting, then finally to my delight, I noticed her. Standing up immediately, she had her back to me, but I could tell it was her by her long, flowing brunette hair.

As I stared at her, she slowly turned around as if realizing that I was there, noticing me. Eyes fixed on one another, we stood staring at each other, smiles forming on our faces, tugging at our cheeks from end to end. She finally lifted her glance off me, motioned something to a few of the children, and said something to one of her colleagues beside her. She began walking towards me, pulling her hair behind her ears and glancing up at me a few times along the way, coyly, as if I didn't notice.

She reached me and we stood face to face. "Hello," we both said at roughly the same time, causing us both to laugh and drop our heads in a moment of innocence and levity.

"Hey," she said to me, "that was quick." I smiled at her and said nothing. "Did you find what you were looking for?" she asked me. If only she knew, I thought to myself.

"Yes, I did," I responded.

"So what brings you back here then?" she asked me.

"I'm not sure," I responded, "I guess it just felt like the right place to be." She nodded, smiling at me while I adored her with my eyes. Just then, we were interrupted by one of the other officials calling her name.

"I'll be right back," she said.

"It's okay, I have to leave," I responded, stopping her in her tracks and drawing a disappointed expression on her face. "For now, that is, I have to go for now."

"Oh, okay," she said.

"Meet me for coffee tonight when you're done. Same place. Same time?" I asked her. "She didn't respond." There are some things I'd like to share with you," I qualified.

"Okay," she quietly whispered from under her soft lips. "I'll see you tonight then."

"Okay, great," I responded.

"I have to go now," she said, gesturing to the field officer who called her once more.

"Of course," I said as I nodded and she walked away. I had deliberated much about whether I would tell her what I knew now, about her past, her beginnings. She had a right to know the truth, heavy as it may be. I really had no choice in the end, because if there was one thing I had learned on this journey of mine that had brought me face to face with my life and my truth, it was this: though the truth may travel a thousand miles, and visit a hundred places, it will always find its way home.

She would one day find out, so it was best that it be from me. I turned around and began the long walk back to the main building, excited to have my moment with her later tonight.

I had made my way to the meeting area earlier. I wanted to cross the bridge and stand in between the Bosphorous River and take in all of Istanbul, from above the water. It was as exhilarating as I had expected it to be. The sun was setting slowly and the brisk wind caressed my face. I would be forever tied to this place, and depending on how things played out with her, I might well end up spending significantly more time here. Could I move here, I thought to myself now? It was, after all, just another city, like Toronto, London or New York. I had grown weary of those places, but I realized that my problems were not so much about place, but purpose. I simply felt that my life lacked purpose and meaning back there. It seemed as though everyone simply lived to work, make money and spend it on things they didn't need, or need so much of. This can't be the high purpose of a human life, it will never lead to happiness. After everything that had happened to me, I had realized something. We have the freedom and ability to choose how we live and what we do with our lives. We needn't mindlessly go along with everything and everyone that surrounds us. Why stay at a job you hate, or lease something you can't afford just to keep up appearances? Why consume alcohol or drugs just to escape reality? Why does reality require an escape at all?

Then again, perhaps it was even simpler than all this. Perhaps it's just about finding love. That's the Holy Grail, isn't it, finding that right person to go through life with? What did I know about it considering my past? I did however know intimately well that where one door closes, another usually opens. That all is not lost. The world is abundant. I had lost my father, but had found truth. I had lost Anastasya, but had found Kanda. Who knows what rhyme and reason exists in all the things that happen to us everyday? All I knew at this moment was that a better life does exist, that there is indeed a reason why everything happens, and that anything at all is possible. Whatever we are looking for, it is out there, we can find it; we must first simply look. Really and truly look. And probably make some sacrifices and take some risks.

I was walking up the hill towards the café, when to my great delight, I saw her standing at the entrance. She wasn't looking in my direction, but I stared at her all the way.

"Hello," I said to her, surprising her as she turned to me and smiled.

"Hello again."

I looked at the doorway with several people filling it. "What's the matter here?" I asked.

"They are just busy, soccer match on."

It would be loud then inside, I surmised. "Well, how about another spot? I'm sure you know several in these parts."

She paused for a moment and looked away. "Yes, there is a quaint little wine bar just down that way along the water," she said, pointing past me.

I smiled. "That will be perfect."

We had been walking 10 minutes or so and I had given her the outline of why I had gone to Kiev and Tehran. She already knew I was on a quest for information about my father. She listened to what I had to tell her, and finally asked me a question. "Why did you return here? What is it that you have to tell me?" It was done in a sweet, shy sort of way, like when someone is asking a question that concerns themselves, but act as though it's really about you.

I stopped and so did she. We faced one another. I wasn't quite sure how to respond, or begin to tell her. Should I tell her? I thought to myself, perhaps its best left unsaid. What if she can't look at me the same once I do? What if she simply isn't even drawn to me, but pities me or hates me? The various scenarios went about in my mind as I stared at this beautiful young lady who now held my heart.

"Well," she said to me, finally disturbing my thoughts, "tell me, why are you back and what do you want from me?"

I was a bit caught off guard by it. "I am not ready to go back home yet," I said. "I'm not even sure if that is home any longer."

She looked at me curiously, tilting her head ever so slightly that a thin strand of her supple hair swung across her face.

"How about your family, your work, your friends?"

Yes, what about these things, I thought to myself.

"I can work anywhere," I responded quickly, not much caring for that part. "Family and friends, I'll always be close to them and see them regularly. You can never really lose those things anyways."

She stared at me, seeming reserved. "I see. Well, it must be nice to be able to just do that, to up and leave and go as you please, leaving those in your life behind." Was she insinuating something?

"Well, it's not that…" I began to say, but was quickly interrupted.

"So what did you have to tell me anyways? Do you want to know what I found out about your father?" I had forgotten about that. What did it matter anymore? She seemed a bit upset.

"Kanda, what's wrong?" I asked her.

She waved her head and said, "Nothing. Forgive me. I'm just tired."

"It's quite fine," I responded. "Are we near it?"

"Yes, it's just a couple minutes down there."

I turned to look in the direction she was pointing to. "Great, well, let's keep walking then."

As soon as I turned my body around, she grabbed my right arm, turning me back around to face her.

"What did you have to tell me?"

I looked at her. She clearly wanted to know before we went any further. It surprised me that she was this sensitive and eager. Perhaps she had after all fallen for me and was worried I merely needed her for my purposes? Perhaps she had been hurt before by other men? Perhaps I could not, should not tell her after all? All our lives, we often hesitate when there is something or someone there before us that we want, scared that perhaps we might be rejected or fail.

Looking at her, this beautiful, soft person with a twinkle in her round, dotted eyes, I wanted nothing more than to kiss her and embrace that powerful feeling, if only once more. I stepped forward, one foot after the other as she stared deep into my eyes. I brought my head toward hers, tilting it slightly while our eyes dotted around each other's faces as if a bee looking for the right spot on the flower to land. Finally, our eyes closed and our lips connected. Hers were soft and moist like warm chocolate. She smelled of spring.

Placing one hand across her lower back and the other cupping her shoulder blades, I brought her closer to me as we embraced more passionately, like soldiers do their women upon returning home from war. She gave herself to me fully, and for a moment, we blended into one another like pictures in a reel of film. I slowly released my hold on her and pulled my lips away gently as she just stood there, eyes closed. When she finally opened them, I could tell she felt just as I did. The eyes never lie, and lips always confirm what the heart has spoken. I had never quite felt as I did at just this moment before, with anyone, and that's how I knew.

She smiled, unable to peel her eyes off me. "Who are you?" she whispered. If she only knew, I thought to myself.

"I have something important to tell you," I said to her gently. I put my hand out and she extended hers and grabbed it. I held it and motioned for her to walk with me. "Let's sit down and I will tell you who I am… and who you are."

About the Author

Massoud Abbasi was born in 1982, in Tehran, Iran. His family fled war to Turkey in 1987, where they were refugees, until arriving in Canada 1989. He holds a BComm, BA Philosophy and an MBA in Finance from McMaster University. A successful finance professional and aspiring philanthropist, he is an increasingly influential public figure in Toronto. Upon the death of his father in 2013, a writer and journalist, he became inspired to follow in his footsteps and pursue his own passion and lifelong dream of becoming a writer. He left his job and began penning his debut novel, Seeker of Horizons.

Made in the USA
Charleston, SC
25 April 2014